Return
of the
Scream
Queen

Michael McCarty – Linnea
Quigley – Stan Swanson

BLACK BED
SHEET

Return of the Scream Queen
A Black Bed Sheet/Diverse Media Book
February 2025

ISBN 10: 1-946874-68-X
ISBN 13: 978-1-946874-68-9

Return of the Scream Queen

A Black Bed Sheet/Diverse Media Book
Antelope, CA

♥

Dedicated to the memory of Chuck Acri and Acri Creature Feature (and Michael McCarty was once a "Creep of the Week") and late great movie screenwriter and director Dan O'Bannon.

Michael McCarty

Special thanks to:

The lovely Linnea Quigley, Stan Swanson. The Amazing Kreskin, Holly Zaldivar, Larry Nadolsky, Christopher & Valerie Miron, Thomas Piccirilli. Tammy Pescatelli, Kimberly Cole Zemke, Svengoolie Marlena Midnite & *Midnite Mausoleum*, *Cemetery Dance* Publications, Black Bed Sheet Books and my enchanting wife Cindy McCarty…

Linnea Quigley

Special thanks to:

Mom, Dad, my collaborator horrormeister Michael McCarty, my animal companions and to all the witches in the world….

Stan Swanson

Special thanks to:

My co-authors, Mike McCarty and Linnea Quigley for inviting me aboard and also to my lovely wife who has always encouraged me to keep writing.

☼ ACKNOWLEDGMENTS:

The Skirts, Jody LaGreca, Jean Brandt, Mel Piff, Chef Steph, Joe McKinney, The Book Rack, The Source Book Store, The Brewed Book, Obsidian & Sage, Cheri, Brian Kilgore, Dave and Julie Thompson, the memory of Latte the Bunny, the memory of Kitty the Bunny, Scott Thomas Trimble, Veronique Fernandez, The McCarty Family, The Quigley Family, PETA, Trena, Alan Spencer, Patricia Esposito, Kali Maddox, R.L. Fox, Bonnie, Bonnie Delight, Brian Kronfeld, Quinn & Iggy & Brian Kronfeld, Leslie Langtry and such filmmakers as: David DeCoteau, Fred Olen Ray, Kevin Tenney, Quentin Tarantino Robert Rodriguez, Tom Savini, Mick & Cynthia Garris, Joe & Crystal Lake Entertainment and of course Nicholas Grabowsky and Black Bed Sheet Books.

PRAISE FOR *RETURN OF THE SCREAM QUEEN*

"Sequel to *Night of the Scream Queen*, a tribute to B movie horror, as is this follow up. This one is subtitled *"Embrace of the Aztec Vampire"*, which sort of tells you what the story is about. An Aztec queen - did they have queens? - is infuriated when European invaders destroy her civilization, and she's back from the dead to have revenge on the present. And she's not human any more. A scream queen is the perhaps unlikely protagonist who has to rise to the occasion and prevent the apocalypse. This is not to be taken entirely seriously, of course, just as most of the movies in this sub-genre are at least partly tongue in cheek. Fun particularly for those of us who still feel the compulsion to watch cheaply made and usually awful horror movies."
-Critical Mass Reviews
by Don D'Ammassa

"With *Night of the Scream Queen*. Linnea Quigley and Michael McCarty have penned one of my favorite guilty pleasure novels of the year. This is over-the-top good fun, the way they used to make it down at the drive in. I loved it, and I bet you will too. Highly recommend!"
-Joe McKinney, Bram Stoker Award-winning author of
The Dead Won't Die, Flesh Eaters* and *Apocalypse of The Dead

"I have just read *Night of the Scream Queen* by Linnea Quigley and Michael McCarty. Never have descriptive words such as zany, irreverent and outlandish been more appropriate. It is an outrageous satire of horror fiction both in cinema and print, the likes of which I have never read before. It makes the casts in Tod Browning's Freaks seem tame! This is one of the wildest books I've ever read."

-The Amazing Kreskin

"*Night of the Scream Queen* resurrects movie monsters of yesteryear and breathes new life into the genre. Michael McCarty and Linnea Quigley deliver thrills and chills that will leave their readers gasping for more."

-Amy Grech, Author of *Rage & Redemption in Alphabet City* and *Blanket of White*

"B-Movie Energy! I read this bad boy in one sitting. Being a fan of b-movies in general, the story involving b-movie actors, b-movie filmmakers, and gator people, I ate this right up. You have to be okay with the ridiculous (and fun) premise, or else stick with straight-laced fiction. It's geared more towards humor, so if you're ready to laugh, pop open a cool one and enjoy. Also, I really really enjoyed the snippets about Desiree Starr's movie experiences before each chapter. Fun, fun stuff!"

-Alan Spencer author of *B-Movie Wars* and *Psycho Therapy*

"Quirky, yummy fun! Michael McCarty and Linnea Quigley had me at '*Blood Brothel Mama*' Read the book!"

-Leslie Langtry author of *Mud Run Murder* and *Stand by Your Hitman*

Table of Contents:

Introduction

B-Movie Participant
by Alan Spencer

"I have a special requirement when giving cheesy horror movies the thumbs up. Most people consider monsters, gore and nudity, and a wild premise enough to be won over. Me, I expect one other thing. At some point during the viewing process, I should wish to be in the actual film. I know it sounds crazy. If you entered a horror movie in progress, the odds are, you're going to die, and it's not going to be pretty. Let me explain. I swear I don't have a death wish.

First, I should narrow down the playing field. What do I mean by "cheesy" horror movies? I don't want people thinking I want to exist in *Cannibal Holocaust* or a brutal film like *Martyrs*. Good movies, but yikes, I'd probably die in the first few minutes without having a single taste of fun. Imagine this. When the dorky guys are forced to join in on a sorority prank at a bowling alley in *Sorority Babes in the Slimeball Bowl-O-Rama*, consider me the guy breaking the lock to get into that bowling alley. I'd love to be the detective in *Hollywood Chainsaw Hookers* who deals with a string of brutal murders, while being stalked by bodacious (and chainsaw wielding) nubile women. I would jump at the chance to dress up for Halloween and join the teenagers entering a haunted house on Halloween night in *Night of the Demons*. Before combating demons and zombies, I'd be granted forty-five minutes of playing pranks and dancing with that hot goth chick before being '86'd. And don't forget jamming out with the killer from *Slumber Party Massacre II*. This dude rocks out with a Drill-tar. Yes, you read right. That's a guitar with a drill coming out the neck of the instrument. I'd love to get music lessons from that guy! After learning up, I'd really know how to shred on some licks.

What I'm trying to say is a great cheesy movie provides fun and antics even before the slaughter begins. The characters are always up to things you wish you'd done in high school, college, or later on in your adult years but never had the situation to live them through. I want to be there or even if chances are when the party is over, I'm going buy the farm. And even up to the point of death, I'm yucking it up all the way to the grave.

Life can be monotonous. Work. Paying bills. Whatever. But you take that normality and throw in all the great tidbits of horror cheese and wild characters, and suddenly, your life is so much more exciting. It's a party. This is what I experienced in massive doses while reading *Return of the Scream Queen*. I want to hang out with Desiree Starr and her bevy of fellow actors, agents, and bedfellows. It's so enjoyable I don't fear horror's reprisal. A gator-guy might chomp me to bits. A well-endowed Aztec vampire might sink her sumptuous teeth into my neck, but so what? It's all good and I had a wonderful time being attacked and thank you for the opportunity!

Part One

Evil Whispers

"From the pool a green hand rises,
But does it scare us or surprise us?
Not if you're the queen of screams,
Who simply laughs at childish schemes."
-Stan Swanson

I

Stay the Night

It was one of those days that a tourist would find hot and hazy. A day for a trip to Grauman's Chinese Theatre or Madame Tussauds. Anything to stay out of the heat. But for Southern California residents, it was just another typical hot and lazy summer afternoon.

Desiree Star had dealt with the desert for years and usually conquered it by lying in her shaded pool on her pink plastic raft. Both plastic armrests on the raft were filled. One held her Cell phone and the other a half empty Margarita glass. (Very little ice, a heavy load of salt around the rim and plenty of Tequila.) Her laptop rested on her bare stomach and a half dozen movie scripts were within arm's reach between her thighs.

The Santa Annas blew the smog to another part of the planet for a change, and she breathed in the hot breezy balmy air that carried a hint of jasmine from her neighbor's flowering shrubs. The old man next door gave her the creeps and Donald told her that he thought he might be a Peeping Tom, but he sure took good care of his garden and shrubbery.

Finding that her brain refused to kick in, she closed the laptop and reached for the scripts. She really didn't want to do another horror movie, this one with the title *The Slime Creature Rises Again*. She didn't even know the Slime Creature rose at all. If she played her card rights, maybe she wouldn't have to watch any slimier or creature movies anymore. But her mother in Iowa had always told her, "If you jump out of a plane, be sure you have a second parachute, just in case the first one doesn't open." As much as she hoped that *Bullet City* would become a big hit, nothing was for sure in this crazy town. But doing another horror movie after *Hell's Belles* weighed heavily on her mind. And she didn't even want to think about everything that had happened in the Devil's Bayou. But there were bills to pay after moving into Long Beach condo and it didn't take too long to be forgotten in this dog-eat-dog business. Or was that bitch-eat-bitch business?

Lost in her own world as she paged through one of the scripts, she didn't even notice the ripple in the water off to her left. Long green fingers with razor sharp nails broke the water surface first and was followed by a swamp green slimy hand. The hand reached for the side of her raft, and she broke into laughter.

"Where the hell did you find that?" she asked as Donald rose out of the water. He flashed a sparkling smile (he was a dentist after all) and pushed his peroxide blonde hair from his eyes. Maybe the years were adding up for Desiree Starr, but she still had the power to attract her fair share of 'boy-toys'. And her new boyfriend fit the bill to a tee, tall, dark and brutally handsome. From head to toe as well as strategic spots in between.

He smiled and wiggled the fingers of the prop.

Desiree laughed. "Is that the creature's claw from *Monster from the Murky Lake*?"

"Hell, if I know, I think that was before my time," he replied with another grin.

"Donny, stop that. You're going to make me feel old. Besides, it was made," she paused. "Well, it wasn't before your time."

"Just playing with you," Donald replied. He was practically naked as the only thing covering his body was a white Speedo swimsuit. He enjoyed showing off his well-toned, muscular, twenty-nine-year-old body. Desiree just hoped he wasn't sharing it with anyone else. You never knew about that in Hollywood either.

He swam to the edge of the pool and climbed out knowing that Desiree 's eyes were glued to the water running off his back and thighs. He threw a beach towel around his neck and tossed the monster glove on a wicker table next to the cabana.

"Where did you find that thing?" she asked.

"It was stuffed in the bottom of one of those boxes in the spare bedroom," he said.

"And just what were you doing going through my things?" she asked in jest.

"Just looking for a pair of panties to sell on eBay," he said, and she wasn't sure if he was kidding or not. "But all those memorabilia you have might be worth some money, doll. Your condo is like a regular Planet Hollywood or should I say Planet Horror-wood. Did you steal props and clothes from every film you've even been in?"

"I didn't steal anything," she said with a pout. "They were either given to me or I dug them out of the trash as souvenirs."

"Is that same black and white striped bikini, you're wearing from one of your movies?" he asked as he sat down at the edge of the pool with a fresh drink in his hand. "I think I recognize it."

"I don't think so. I bought this from one of those shops on Melrose a few summers ago. Besides, I don't think I could even fit into most of those bikinis I wore back then. That was ages ago."

"Ages?" he asked seductively cocking an eyebrow.

"Well," the Scream Queen gulped. "I mean a few years. Besides, I don't think it's my bikini you're staring at. Anyway, I really want to be done with that horror movie image and all those crazy monsters."

"Even the monster in my Speedos," he asked with an evil grin.

***

Nightfall and Santa Annas made the evening balmy and breezy. They had enjoyed a nice dinner in the Valley and then drove to Dr. Donald Becker's house in Brentwood. He didn't even bother to park the Bentley in the garage as they hurried inside, clothes coming off as fast as they could climb the stairs to his bedroom.

It was quick, but intense and they were both soon lying naked and wrapped around another's sweaty bodies that glistened in the shimmering moonlight.

She wondered if he was already asleep until he spoke. "You really think you're done with movies like *Count Dracula and His Satanic Sluts* and *Blood Brothel Mama*?"

Desiree thought about it for a moment. Summer was melting away faster than ice in a margarita glass and fall was just around the corner. And in her world, that meant she was going to be bombarded with invitations to appear at too many second-rate horror conventions and receive even more horror scripts. Although *Hell's Belles* had not been a first-rate horror film (was there really such a thing anymore?), the publicity surrounding her abduction had earned the film a solid chunk of money. She was in high demand. But if *Bullet City* was super successful; maybe she wouldn't have to worry about horror films anymore.

Not receiving an answer to his question, Donny slid out of the bed and reached for his black, silk robe. He rotated in front of the mirror that also served as the door to his closet. (As well as a nice view of the bed.)

"Do you think I look like Tom Cruise," he asked seemingly out of the blue.

"Huh? What?" Desiree asked, caught by surprise by the offhand comment.

"Do you think I could pass for a Tom Cruise clone? I've had tourists stop me on the street and ask me if I was Tom Cruise. If I appeared in a film, do you think people would believe it was Tom Cruise and not me?"

"I guess I never really thought about it," she told him as she slipped into her pink kimono. She studied her boyfriend a little closer and even squinted her eyes. "Sure, I guess you resemble him a little."

He smiled. "If *Bullet City* becomes a hit, do you think you could get me a small part in the sequel? Maybe even speak a few lines?"

"Donny, darling, you're a dentist, not an actor."

"Hey, I had a walk-in role in *Bullet City*."

"Donny. You were an extra. You stood and held a newspaper on a busy intersection while bullets were being fired down the street. They had to keep on reshooting it because you kept dropping the newspaper because you heard gunfire."

"Well," he huffed. "You must start somewhere. You're not the only one with big dreams, you know."

"Yeah, sorry. I didn't mean it that way."

"Do you know Tom Cruise only had a few lines in his first movie *Endless Love*? And now he's one of the biggest stars in the world. I've even been practicing sounding like him. Maybe I could start as his body double or something. He is getting a little older, you know. Listen to this—"

He turned from the mirror and winked. "—Mission Possible. We just rolled up a snowball and threw it into Hell. Now we'll see if it has a chance."

He curled his thumb and straightened his index finger like a pointed gun and made a 'click click' sound as he flashed his incandescent smile at her.

Desiree thought he sounded more like rock star Tom Petty than the famous actor.

"Uh," the Scream Queen stalled as she tried to think of a nice comment to make. Nothing came to mind, so she lied instead. "Not bad, I guess."

"I knew you'd like it," he said flashing the bright smile again and brimming with way too much confidence.

He scowled as a cell phone lying on the nightstand rang and interrupted his moment in the sun. They both reached for their phones automatically, but the *Mission Impossible* ringtone should have given it away. He glanced at the caller ID before flipping open the phone.

"Dr. Becker," he answered, sounding nothing like Tom Cruise. He listened for a moment, then gave Desiree a look of disappointment before he answered his caller. "One of your caps came loose. Well, I can meet you at my office in about an hour and a half. You realize since it is an emergency visit, it will cost more."

He paused.

"Yes, I'm sorry. I'm aware that money is not an issue. I'll be there in—" he glanced at his watch. "—thirty minutes and you'll be in perfect shape for your red-carpet appearance tonight. I guarantee it. After all, you are my number one patient."

He rolled his eyes at Desiree as he said this and flipped the faceplate shut. "If you haven't already guessed, I have to go into the office for a bit."

"That's okay," Desiree said looking for her bra and then remembering it was on the railing at the top of the staircase. "I need to get back to my condo anyway."

"You don't want to stay the night?" he asked as he gave her his familiar hurt puppy dog look.

"Too much to do, darling," she said as she retrieved her bra. "I have an interview scheduled for tomorrow and then need to work on *Memoirs of a Scream Queen*. The publisher is getting a little frantic over it. And don't you dare forget that the premiere of *Bullet City* is tomorrow night. You are still going, right?"

"You betcha! Wouldn't miss it for the world," he said giving her a kiss on the forehead. "It's going to be *Top Gun* fun," he said, this time sounding just a little more Tom Cruise-ish and a little less Tom Petty-ish.

"Morning on the beach
Orange sun reflected in the waves
Solitude and the sand
Headache from the midnight-rave"
-Michael McCarty

II

The Interview

Desiree woke to the bombastic blast of the hard rock band Led Zeppelin who were accompanied with an Eastern string section in the song "Kashmir." She immediately hit the off button on the alarm. She wasn't a huge heavy metal fan, but she found that if she turned the radio to a jazz or light rock station then she usually slept right through it and today she had too much on her plate to sleep late.

She stretched, trying to work the kinks of a restless night from her system. She knew immediately that she was not at Don's posh house that resembled an antebellum plantation with its Greek massive columns and an unobstructed view of Marilyn Monroe's Brentwood Hacienda. She also knew she was at home in her Long Beach condo as was indicated by the fluffy clouds painted on her bedroom ceiling.

At least it isn't covered with zombies, mummies and vampires, she thought. One of her longtime Scream Queen friends, Gina Bellarossi, had recommended she paint her ceiling that way after having her own place done in that fashion. Of course, Gina had been sleeping with an 'up-and-coming' artist at the time.

The clouds work just fine, she thought.

And it was no secret that she was beginning to tire of the whole horror scene. Which only fueled her hopes that *Bullet City* be a success.

She walked through the sliding glass doors to her balcony and didn't realize she was still dressed in her slinky pink nightie until she spotted the old perv from next door working in his garden. Only he wasn't staring at his plants. She quickly stepped back inside.

Okay, she thought to herself, 7:30. Time to organize a very busy day.

She knew she had to work out at some point, but wasn't sure where she could fit it in. As the years added up, it became tougher and tougher, but her profession had no allowances and no excuses. The last thing she wanted to do was play someone's mother (or worse, yet grandmother) in some third-rate slasher film.

Her interview with Zach Wawrzyniak from *Monster Agogo Magazine* wasn't until 10:30. Plenty of time for her usual coffee gab session with Gina.

She took a quick shower and debated shaving her legs but figured she would leave that for later in the day so she would be at her absolute best when she showed up for the red-carpet pre-premiere event. She pulled on a pair of black shorts and a *Bullet City* t-shirt before grabbing her dark sunglasses and heading out the door.

Jitters, the local coffee shop, was only a few minutes away so she left her leased Lexus in the garage.

She saw Gina at their usual table in back (away from the front windows in case someone recognized them from the street), waved and ordered her usual cup of coffee which was just slightly smaller than the planet Jupiter.

Gina put down the copy of Leslie Langtry's *Movie Night Murder* she was reading and gave Desiree a hug.

"What?" Desiree asked. "No horror novel today?"

"Just needed a change of pace and I just finished Jeff Strand's *Clowns Vs Spiders* yesterday."

"Nice guy," Desiree said taking a big sip of coffee. "He was at the last convention I attended."

"Excited about the big event tonight?" Gina asked.

"Not sure whether I'm excited, nervous or just plain scared-to-death. But I figure this is my last chance to escape the world of horror."

"Don't know why you want to," her girlfriend replied. "Horror has been good to you."

"I know, but the fact that I was willing to run around half-naked in most of those movies didn't hurt either."

Gina smiled. "Well, it would sure give me more opportunities. I'm reading for *College of the Living Dead* next week. How about you?"

Desiree shrugged. "I guess I've been spouting so many anti-horror rants lately, that they were afraid to send me a script. But I seriously doubt it. Depends a lot on *Bullets* to tell you the truth."

"Speaking of the premiere, did you know that Aimee Breeze from *Entertainment Right Now* is doing the red-carpet interviews tonight?"

"Shit," Desiree said with a pout. "I hate that bee-ech, excuse my French. She's about as plastic as a blowup doll."

Gina laughed, almost spitting out her coffee. "That's a good one."

"That blonde bimbo reporter did everything but spit on my performance in *The Chaperone*. I don't think she likes me very much."

"Everybody loves you, Desi. Even the gators that live in the Florida swamps and the gator guy living in England."

The hairs on Desiree 's arms stood up. "Please, Gina, I really don't want to think about that."

"Sorry. But you have to admit that it put your name back on everyone's list."

Desiree shrugged. "That doesn't mean I'd want it to happen all over again. I really didn't think I was going to make it out of there alive."

"Did you hear about Geoffrey Terronez?"

"No, what?"

"He's being questioned about some of the missing people on the sets of his last two films."

"Wow," Desiree said as she glanced at the time and finished off her coffee. "That's something. I always thought there was something strange about the guy. I always loved his work, but it always seemed a little bit too real. Of course, he is in the business of horror, and they are a kooky and spooky bunch."

"Well, he's just being questioned at this point," Gina said. "He probably hires some high-priced attorney and get off."

"Guess I should listen to the news more often," Desiree said as she reached for her bag. "Well, I hate to drink and run, my luv, but it's a busy day. You gonna be around tonight? Maybe you and I and Don and whoever your current barely-of-age female plaything is, can go out for drinks after the premiere. And, hopefully, we'll have something to celebrate."

"Sounds good," Gina said.

"And don't stare at my butt as I walk out the door."

"I can't make any promises, Desi," Gina said with a smile and didn't move her eyes from Desiree 's ass until a blonde with big breasts walked in.

***

It had been years since Desiree had visited the offices of *Monster Agogo Magazine*. The lobby was old and not as well maintained as it had been at one time. There wasn't even a receptionist at the front desk.

Time takes its toll on us all, Desiree thought.

She heard footsteps from down the hallway and turned.

A tall man dressed entirely in black walked towards her. He hadn't changed much since the last time she'd seen him. He still looked like a cross between Santa Claus and the guy from *The Texas Chainsaw Massacre*. You didn't know whether to hug the man or chop off his head with a machete.

"Hello Red," he said gazing at her over the top of his Elton John glasses.

"Hey, Zach," she replied. "How's it going? Getting any?"

He laughed. Despite his looks, Zach Wawrzyniak got his fair share of the ladies. It amazed Desiree, but it just went to show that looks weren't everything. Of course, it didn't hurt that he could help a girl's career along with a good article in the magazine either.

"It has been a long time," the man said with a huge grin, "But you still look great. And *Hell's Belles* proved you still have what it takes, my love."

"Times rough in the magazine business, Zach?"

"Well, the print edition doesn't sell many copies. I think we'll shut it down soon. But the online version does pretty good. We get over a quarter of a million hits per week."

Desiree smiled. "You know, your magazine was the first cover I ever appeared on."

He laughed. "Took a little air-brushing to make sure people didn't think we were a soft porn magazine. Let's go into my office, okay. More comfortable and the air-conditioning actually works in there."

They walked down the hall to his office. She heard voices down the hall, so she knew there were other employees still working for the magazine. But the world of electronics had changed everything, and she wasn't sure it was all for the good.

"You okay with me videotaping this so we can stream it on the website?"

She shrugged. "No problem. Just make sure you get my good side."

He glanced down at her chest and smiled. "No problem." He adjusted the camcorder and hit record.

"Good morning, Miss Starr. It's been a while since we've interviewed you. Thank you for coming down and sharing a few moments with us."

"Glad to do it," she replied. "I've always been a big fan of the magazine."

"It's been twenty years since you appeared in *Monster from The Murky Lake* which is still one of the biggest and most popular movies you ever appeared in."

"Has it been that long since that movie came out?" she asked as she did the math in her head. "I guess it has. Wow. Now that's scary."

Zach grinned. "And now you're ready for the big time with the world premiere of *Bullet City* tonight."

"Well, we'll see," she replied. "I think it has a real chance."

"So, are you done with horror?"

"Not at all. I can't desert my fan base like that. I'll admit that the last few movies I've done weren't horror films, but that doesn't mean I won't do another one down the road. Tina Hamilton gave me some solid roles in *The Chaperone* which was a romantic comedy where I played the chaperone of a Miss USA contest and then a made-for-cable version of *Madame Bovary*. I was actually nominated for an Ace Award for that one but lost to Julia Roberts -- that bee-ech." She laughed. "Just joking Julia, let's do lunch sometime. I am hoping that *Bullet City* could be the big one. It was fun working with Colin Hanks."

"No zombies hiding in the alleys?"

Desiree laughed. "Sorry. It's an action adventure."

"Is it true that Tom Hanks has a cameo in the movie as a gangster."

"I'm not at liberty to tell you that, Zach. You'll just have to watch the film at midnight and see for yourself."

"If *Bullet City* is a success, do you think people will always remember you for your Scream Queen parts in all of the horror flicks you've done?"

"Probably," Desiree admitted. "And that's fine. But just because you've fried your eggs all of your life, doesn't mean you can't try making a soufflé."

"Do you realize you have appeared in over fifty movies during your career?"

"Guess I never really counted," she replied with a forced laugh. "Now that's a real horror scenario."

"*Monster from the Murky Lake* turned out to be a classic. Why do you think that was, considering that the movie was done with such a low budget and had no stars in it?"

"What do you mean 'no stars? Aren't you forgetting I was in it, sweetie?"

It was Zach's turn to laugh.

"But twenty years later and it still plays the midnight movie circuit in theaters."

"It was a very sick and twisted movie," she said. "Especially for that time. And it was shot in less than a month. There were a lot of production problems, and it seemed like each of the troubles only made the film scarier. It was also one of Geoffery Terronez's first movies for which he did special effects. He was as responsible for that film's success as much as anyone. He did an incredible job with the lake monster."

"Ah, yes, Mr. Terronez. We tried to get a comment from him about his recent legal problems, what are your thoughts? Do you think he is guilty?"

"Sorry, Zach, but no comment."

"Do you think you could him to do an interview with me?"

"I will give you his contact info after the interview."

"Excellent. So, *Monster from the Murky Lake* was your second film. What was your first?"

"My first was *He Knows When You Are Naked*. I only had one line, ran around in a skimpy bath robe and screamed a lot." She laughed. "I guess that isn't much different from most of the horror films I did."

"Wasn't Candy Sweet originally scheduled to play that part?"

"Ah, Candy. Did you know her name was originally Bertha Hinderschmitt? Anyway, the producer of *Monster* was also the producer of *He Knows When You Are Naked*."

"Leo Irwin Jr., right?"

Desiree nodded. "He really liked my performance and invited me to read for a supporting role. Before filming began, Candy found out she was pregnant and dropped out of the picture. Leo offered me the role of reporter Lisa Youngblood. And, as they say, the rest they say is history."

"What's your secret for continuing to look so great? Do your zombie exercise videos have anything to do with that?"

She laughed. "Thank you. I try to stay in shape. And, by the way, *Desiree Star 's Zombie Workout* is now out on DVD and Blu-ray. It was originally released on VHS."

"Well, you still look good enough to eat, Desiree."

"Well, Zach, I hope you mean that in the nicest sense. At least you are not a zombie," she replied with a wink.

He laughed and briefly touched her knee. "Well, my love, I can assure you I am definitely not a zombie. Anything else you'd like to share with your fans or folks trying to make a go of it here in La La Land?"

"People should not be so hard themselves if they are trying to get into showbiz. There will be people who will try to take you down because they are going down. You've just got to keep your confidence up and be around people who are positive and good. I'd also like to take this opportunity to thank all the fans who have stuck with me over the years. I couldn't have done it without you."

"You'll never know what you'll find
On the corner of SM and Vine
You'll never know what you'll do
When your guy likes boys instead of you
Santa Monica Blvd. Boys."
-Linnea Quigley

III

Midnight Premiere

Desiree drove her Lexus into the garage and hit the garage door remote to close the door behind her. She was glad she could enter her Long Beach condo directly from the garage.

The mid-season heat was an actresses' worst nightmare. She had spent two hours having her hair done at Flavio's on the Boulevard and was nervous that the humidity might play havoc with it. There was also nothing quite like wearing layers of make-up and then sweating like a pig. Oh, that's right, she mused, girls don't sweat, they glow. Bloody hell to whoever came up with that one.

And the two strenuous hours she had spent doing Pilates, cardio and step aerobics earlier that day had certainly done more than made her "glow".

Even in the shade of the garage she could feel the heat.

The dog days of summer might still be a pup, she could still hear her father say, but right now the bitch is panting like an old dog.

It was already noon and although the red-carpet event was scheduled for late evening and still hours away, her afternoon schedule seemed to demand she find a way to develop a clone to help her get everything done. Ah, if wishes were horses, then beggars would ride, she heard her father's voice again. But at least it made her smile to think of him. She had always been close to both of her parents who now lived in Florida.

She spent the next two hours on the phone with the studio and her manager had set up as part of the promotional campaign for *Bullet City*. Although the interviews were limited to just a few minutes each, they seemed to stretch on forever. It was fun at first. Especially with the major media outlets. But by the time she finished her interview with some freelance reporter representing the *Central Kansas Gazette*, it was beginning to take its toll.

She was trying to determine whether to knock out a few more pages of *Memoirs of a Scream Queen* when her cell phone demanded her attention. She held her breath as she flipped it open, hoping that it wasn't another interview.

It was Don. "Hey, love. How's the nerves holding up?"

She smiled, the call brightening the already long day. "Oh, Donald, it's so good to hear your voice. I wish my hair wasn't already done or I'd invite you over for some afternoon delight."

"No problem, chickadee," he replied. "Something came up that demands my attention any way."

"Not another dental emergency, I hope," she said. "I want you looking your best tonight in front of all those cameras."

He laughed. "No, nothing like that. But can the limo driver pick me up at my place instead of me driving to Long Beach?"

"Sure," she replied. "I don't see why not. The studios paid for everything. Who cares about a few extra dollars in gas money?"

He sent her a smooching sound over the phone and hung up.

Desiree yawned and longed to lay down for a nap but knew she couldn't because her hair was already done. She sat down at her laptop and stared at the next blank page of her memoir. The next thing she knew she had fallen asleep in front of the computer and only woke to the buzz of her cell phone. She noticed the screen of her laptop filled with the letter "W" as she had fallen asleep with her hands on the keyboard. She shook sleep from her foggy brain and answered the phone.

"Miss Starr?" It took her a moment to recognize the voice of Richard Schwartz, the executive producer of *Bullet City*.

"Oh, Mr. Schwartz. Is there something wrong?" Why else

would he be calling her? Had they pulled the plug on the movie at the last moment? Her fears were not entirely irrational. Her years in the movie industry had made her a strong believer in the "glass-was-always-half-empty" theory.

"No, no," he assured her. "I just wanted to say thank you for all of your hard work and to wish us all luck tonight."

Desiree sighed with relief and hoped he hadn't heard it. "Thank you, sir. I am really looking forward to this."

"Quite a change from zombies and mummy movies, isn't it?"

"Yes, sir. And I want to thank you again for this opportunity."

"You know," he said after a brief pause. "We should get together next week at my townhouse and discuss some future development projects. We have some meaty roles available which could be just as lucrative as *Bullet City.*"

Desiree knew exactly what that meant, there was no reading between the lines here, the producer was putting his moves on her. "That is a fine idea, but I'm going to Vegas for a couple week vacation, much needed R&R."

"Have fun and don't be a stranger. Give me a ring sometime," he said before ending the call.

After a quick Cajun chicken salad for dinner (she didn't want to collapse on the runway because nothing was in her stomach), she spent nearly an hour on her make-up and then dressed in her new spaghetti-strap black gown and put on her best CFM high heels. All this for five minutes on the red carpet and then to sit in a dark theater where no one will see you for two hours. Of course, there was always the party afterwards. Hopefully it would be a happy gathering and not one of those somber affairs where everyone realized from the audience's reaction that they had a bomb on their hands. Of course, she had very high hopes for *Bullet City*, but she said a silent prayer all the same.

***

"You look delicious," Donald whispered into her ear as the limo inched forward in the line of cars arriving at the red-carpet area of the premiere.

"You clean up pretty nice yourself," Desiree said. He looked dashing in his white tuxedo. It would contrast nicely with her slinky black gown, and they'd make a great looking couple as the video streamed live to the *Entertainment Right Now* studios. She cuddled up closer to him, careful not to muss her hair, smear her makeup or wrinkle her dress. It wasn't easy.

He smiled and squeezed her arm. ""You're my everything, baby," he said, giving her a quick kiss, then trying to turn it into a more passionate one.

"Donald! You're gonna smear my lipstick," the Scream Queen complained. "There'll be plenty of time for that later. And what is that smell? If it's some new cologne, then I suggest you change brands. It's much too sweet smelling and spicy. It reminds me of patchouli."

"What?" he asked, his eyebrows rising high on his forehead. "I'm not wearing cologne. I don't know..." He slapped his forehead (reminding Desiree of the V8 commercials) and laughed. "Oh, it must have been that incense I lit earlier while I was, er... meditating."

"Since when did you start meditating, Donald?"

He seemed irritated. "What difference does it make? We're next in line in case you hadn't noticed."

She shrugged and thought nothing more about it. Her big moment was arriving. Someone opened the limo door for them and helped Desiree step out onto the red carpet, the entire area bathed in bright lights. She imagined herself tripping and falling straight on her face on national television and clung even tighter to her boyfriend.

"Look," she whispered as they headed up the walk towards a set of stairs leading to the interview area. "It's Aimee Breeze. If I start to embarrass myself, give me a jab in the side. She's real snake in the grass."

"Aimee Breeze? You're kidding me. She's doing the interviews tonight?" He paused and she jerked his arm to get him moving again.

"Yes," Desiree replied. "Dreadful, isn't it? But we're gonna look great up there, sweetie. Come on. We don't want to keep her waiting."

"Oh, damn," he said as he patted his pants pocket. "I think I dropped my wallet in the limo. Sorry."

"Donald!"

"I'll be right back," he promised. "Go ahead and do your interview. I have to catch that driver before he gets too far away down the line."

She frowned, her lips turning down in one of her infamous pouts which were usually reserved for the movies. "Fine. Hurry up, please. I really don't want to face that creature without you."

He shrugged and hurried away as she made her way up the steps towards the interview area where Aimee Breeze was just finishing her interview with one of the minor actors from the movie.

She hesitated and looked back, but then Aimee was speaking into her microphone and the cameraman swiveled the camera in her direction. "And here is one of the stars of *Bullet City*, Desiree Starr. What a lovely gown you are wearing."

"Thank you," Desiree said sounding as polite as she knew how. "It is a Jordan Jardin."

"Desiree, I expected to see you on the arm of some handsome man tonight. Sorry you had to go it alone." Aimee Breeze smirked as she spoke the words.

Desiree smiled politely, but a curious expression came across her face. "Oh, I'm not alone. My boyfriend will be along momentarily. You know, that's an interesting perfume you are wearing."

Aimee was caught off-guard. "What? Oh, my perfume. Very expensive, Desiree. It probably isn't in your price range. It's Ralph Lauren's Romance perfume. The fragrance has a lot of patchouli." She winked into the camera. "Supposed to have some aphrodisiac properties. We'll see after the party."

"Patchouli?"

"Yes, my dear," the reporter replied. "I know it's a big word. Oh, forgive me Desiree. I must move along. I see my boyfriend in the crowd, and I know he would love some screen time. He's dying to be an actor."

Desiree turned and looked to the area Aimee was motioning towards. She breathed a sigh of relief when she saw Donald in the crowd. Having him at her side would make the evening so much better and maybe she wouldn't look like such a loser in Aimee Breeze's eye. Not to mention the entire TV audience that was watching.

Aimee and Desiree called out at the same time.

"Donald!" they shouted in unison and then turned to stare at each other as the realization set in.

"You and Donald?" Aimee whispered as she glanced out of the corner of her eye at the camera.

"You and Donald...?" Desiree repeated.

Donald was trying to disappear into the crowd, but there were just too many people pressing forward. Aimee Breeze forgot she was on television, let go with several four-letter words and then stomped down the carpet. Desiree stayed right behind her as the cameraman desperately tried to keep everything in frame.

The reporter stomped up to a wild-eyed Donald, oblivious to the cameraman still trying to do his job. "You are two-timing bastard," she spat venomously.

"I can explain, baby," he muttered trying to ignore the fact that Desiree was just a few feet away. He lowered his voice to a whisper, but the microphone still held tightly in Aimee's hand picked up every word. "You're my everything, remember–" He didn't have a chance to finish the sentence before Aimee slapped him across the face.

While the slap stunned Donald, it brought the reporter back to reality and she turned towards to the camera, trying to regain her composure. "Uh, more from the red-carpet premiere of *Bullet Town* or whatever the name of this stupid movie is when we come back from commercial."

She dropped the microphone to the carpet and quickly stomped off the interview set as tears welled up in her eyes.

Desiree ignored her retreat and stared at Donald, trying to keep the tears from her own eyes.

"How could you?" she asked softly. "You were the one, Donald. I really thought you were the one..."

She thought about duplicating Aimee's Breeze's slap to his face, but then reconsidered. I'm better than that, she thought and followed Aimee Storm off the set leaving Donald standing there alone, the cameraman still pointing the camera at him. Thinking fast, he realized a national television audience was watching and that his possible moment of fame might be at hand. He flashed his brilliant smile and said, "Uh, Mission Possible?"

Unfortunately for Donald Becker, the network had already cut to a commercial for erectile dysfunction.

***

Desiree headed straight for the nearest lady's room. She had no longer been able to contain the tears and she feared she now looked like a raccoon with the mascara and eye shadow running down her face. She prayed that Aimee Breeze hadn't done the same thing. The bathroom was empty, and she said a silent 'thank you'.

She managed to make her face look a little less Picasso-like after splashing it with cold water several times. She grabbed several paper towels to dry herself with. Opening her purse, she grabbed a package of tissues, but between more tears and blowing her nose, she quickly ran out.

The door opened and Desiree held her breath in the hope that it wasn't Aimee Breeze. It wasn't, but she was surprised when she recognized Lucretia Terronez entering the bathroom wearing a marvelous white gown and thousands of dollars' worth of diamonds around her neck.

"Lucretia," Desiree managed to say.

"Just call me Lu, all my friends do."

"Okay, Lu, I thought... I thought you were in England."

The beauty smiled. "Leonard and the band are playing at the after-party tonight.

"Leonard?"

"Sewer Rat," she explained. "You know, lead singer for the Dead Corpses?"

"Oh, of course," Desiree replied dabbing a few more tears from her cheeks. "I just never heard anyone call him Leonard before."

Lucretia laughed. "Well, it's just a little difficult for me to call him Sewer Rat, you know. Especially during those times of, well, shall we say passion?"

Desiree had met Lucretia on the set of *Hell's Belles* where she had been an assistant to her brother Geoffrey Terronez and they had always gotten along well. Desiree tossed her last tissue into the trash and tried to wipe her face with the back of her hand.

Lucretia dug into her bag. "I have some extra tissues if you

20

need them. I saw what happened out there. I'm so sorry..."

The Scream Queen nodded and accepted a fresh pack of Kleenex.

"Leonard's upstairs setting up with the band, hon," Lucretia said. "Would you like me to go with you into the theater?"

"Thanks, but I can't go in there after all of this," she said. "I'm think I just want to go home. I'll go out the side entrance and call for a cab."

"Don't be ridiculous," Lucretia said. "My driver is still here. Why don't I give you a ride home? No offense, but I'm not a big action film fan any way."

"Are you sure?"

"No problem. Maybe we can even stop somewhere on the way and have an Appletini or two."

***

Just moments after Desiree thought she might never smile again, she did, although it took a little effort.

"Thanks," she said as she gave the tall blonde a tight hug.

"But I might want to talk a little business," Lucretia said. "Besides, it will keep your mind off the stupid male species for a while. Geoffrey's doing a new movie and he mentioned your name a few days ago."

"I heard he was in jail," Desiree said, her eyes finally all cried out—at least for the moment.

"Just for questioning. It's all a big misunderstanding. His lawyer took him home before breakfast. Anyway, he's going to start filming *College of the Living Dead* in just a few weeks, and I think you should read it for the leading role. We both love what you did in *Hell's Belles*."

"I've heard a little about it. One of my best friends is reading for it. I just don't know..."

"Here. Take a copy of the script and at least give it a look. It's about these four people flying across the country in a helicopter during the zombie apocalypse. They run out of fuel and land at a private university that is plagued by zombies. And, of course, since they are at a college, all of the zombies are college students. You have this gory makeup on beautiful young sexy bodies. And, as is his trademark, Geoffrey has some of the most amazing special

21

effects planned."

Unsure what to say, Desiree put the script in her purse. "Well, I guess it's the least I can do to help me out on a terrible night. Now, how about those Appletinis?"

Somehow, they managed to escape without being spotted by a single paparazzi.

"You've been playing these games
Making me quite insane
Time to pull back your reigns
It's a hard life to live"
-*Linnea Quigley*

IV

Bite the Bullet

Desiree Starr was tired of flying. First, the long flight (with three stopovers!) that transported her from LAX to the Florida Keys. She would like to have enjoyed a longer stay with her parents, but when it comes to low budget films, time is money. And most horror movies fell into that category.

She was now on a flight from South Florida to Daytona Beach where a driver was scheduled to pick her up and take her to the campus of Angel Falls University. Although Desiree had spent a lot of time in Florida, she had never heard of the school and. But her mom told her it was a very exclusive school built on the site of an abandoned Spanish fort in the late fifties.

The plane hit a small patch of turbulence and Desiree held her breath. She wasn't afraid of flying, but she wasn't sure how close they were to the Devil's Bayou. Hopefully not close. It was an area she planned on avoiding for a long, long time.

The last three days had been nothing but meetings, phone and video conferences and airline flights. Not to mention a lack of food and sleep. At least she had received a healthy portion of meatloaf, mashed potatoes and corn on the cob while spending the day with her parents. Bless her mother for that meal. It brought back memories of her days growing up in Iowa and made up for every other inconvenience of the trip.

The rest of it was a giant blur that she wanted to forget. The current issue of Hollywood Reporter was in her lap as she tightened her seatbelt as another stream of air buffeted them about. She wanted to look out the window but was afraid she would see nothing but swampland below her.

Instead, she glanced down at the front page of the Hollywood gossip paper.

"*Bullet City* Shoots Blanks" read the banner headline.

And towards the bottom of the page an article titled "Scream Queen Turns Drama Queen" was accompanied by a picture of her running off the red carpet. Of course, there was no picture or even a mention of *Entertainment Right Now* reporter Aimee Breeze or her conduct, apparently tabloid TV protects its own.

Desiree had watched all of the news shows and all of the papers and reviews the next day and thought perhaps it was time to retire. Maybe a condo or nice little bungalow in Palm Beach or Miami, she'd just be a hop, skip and a jump from her parents.

A glass of iced tea (with more than a shake or two of vodka) had eased her pain. Shutting off the TV helped as well. She also shut off her cell phone (after erasing dozens of messages from Donald) and settled down on her davenport sofa. Reaching into her purse for her emergency bottle of Advil, her hand had brushed the script that Lucretia had given her the night before. *College of the Living Dead*. She sighed. "Here we go again," she muttered. She began reading, expecting to hate the script and to eventually add it to the yellowing stack of scripts in her desk drawer.

Two hours later she found that she had read the entire script twice and three days after having one of the worst days of her life (not counting her time in the Devil's Bayou, of course), she found herself 30,000 feet above the southern swamps of Florida reading the script for the hundredth time as she memorized the lines of the lead role of Fly Girl.

It also helped that her agent, Curtis Ballinger, had negotiated her one of the best contracts she had received in many years for any of her horror films. Especially since she had opted to take a share of several points for *Bullet City* instead of a huge advance.

It didn't take her long to realize that she would be lucky to make a dime from what everyone was calling one of the "biggest misfires" of the year. At least the deal for *College of the Living Dead* would keep her in her Long Beach condo for years to come.

Of course, time away from California was also a good thing at this point. The last thing she wanted to think about was the cheating bastard that Donald Backer had been. She hoped his teeth all turned rotten and fell out of his mouth and he end up being a toothless Tom Cruise clone working in the dental field. Now that would be true justice.

She closed her eyes and mumbled her lines from scene 8 where half naked zombies were attacking the student union cafeteria. (At this point in her career, she never questioned why anyone appeared naked during a horror film. It was simply a fact of life.)

"Talking to yourself again, Des?"

Gina Bellarossi sat down in the seat next to her after freshening up in the lavatory.

Desiree smiled. "Just practicing my lines."

Gina stuck out her tongue as if they were sitting in a sandbox in third grade. "Those were gonna be my lines, girlfriend."

"I'm sorry, Gina," Desiree said. "It all happened so quickly."

Gina shrugged. "It's okay. And I really enjoyed meeting your folks. Thanks for inviting me. Besides, someone threatened not to sign their contract until I was promised the part of the college president's secretary. Any idea who that might have been?"

Desiree 's eyes widened in fake surprise. "I have no idea. By the way, just how many movies have you played a secretary in, Gina?"

Gina laughed. "With or without my clothes on?"

Desiree smiled but gripped the seat tightly as the airplane took another slight dip in the sky.

"Don't worry," Gina told her with a pat on the arm. "We're almost there which also means we are not over swampland any longer."

Desiree was the only person she had told the entire story of her time in the Devil's Bayou with the Gator Guy.

"I hear you met up with the whole gang before leaving L.A.?"

"It was so strange," Desiree said. "I usually don't attend those things. I just have my agent negotiate my contracts. But they rented the whole Bistro 3000 restaurant for the occasion. Geoffrey Terronez, his sister, Lucretia, and even the producer Blake Smith was there."

"Is Blake still carrying around that teddy bear?"

"Yup, Mr. Twinks was there. Had his own chair and plate and everything. Even wore sunglasses indoors just like Blake. It was a little creepy. Of course, we are in the business of horror."

"And Terronez in his white silk pajamas?"

"Yeah, he's like the Hef of Horror."

"You'll be working the *Hell's Belles* gang again?"

"Yeah. Michelangelo Desalvo plays Gunner – a gun-nut in the new film, PJ Bottoms is cast as Stacks and Sewer Rat is playing himself – which shouldn't be too much of a stretch, even for him."

Both women laughed. She found it amazing she could still laugh after the disaster of the last couple of days. "It was a great feeling, Gina. It's the best paycheck I've had in years, and they even let me change some of the script. Now if I could just forget about Donald..."

"I know this great hypnotist in Beverly Hills. But your other option is to spend a night with me, and you'll forget you ever liked boys."

"Fat chance," Desiree smirked and this time it was her turn to stick out her tongue at her friend.

At that moment, a middle-aged bald man made his way down the aisle and stopped where the two actresses were sitting.

His face turned slightly red. "Aren't you Desiree Starr?" he asked.

Desiree smiled. "Yes. Are you a fan?"

His face glowed. "For many years, Ms. Starr. Oh, I didn't mean to make it sound like that for many, many years. I'm sorry..."

"Don't worry about it, hon," she replied. "We both know how old I am."

"Well, you sure don't look it," he replied, still flustered. "Could I ask for your autograph?"

Desiree smiled. "Certainly."

"What about me?" Gina pouted half seriously.

The man stared at her for a moment.

Gina took a quick look around, then unbuttoned her blouse. When she opened it, she also revealed she was wearing no bra. "Now do you recognize me?"

The man was speechless for a moment and turned an even

brighter shade of red.

"*Neanderthal Nurses from the Northlands?*" he asked.

Gina smiled. "Give the man a gold star," she said with a wink and slowly buttoned her blouse again.

***

Roland Bannister, President of Angel Falls University for the last seven years, snipped off the end of his Reas Belvedere Cuban cigar (and, yes, it was a real Cuban) and using his diamond-emblazoned lighter, took that first deep taste of smoke, it was a smoke-free campus, but that didn't apply to his office.

He blew a perfect smoke ring as continued spooning with Director of Marketing Rebecca Morton, which he hoped would soon lead to forking with the busty blonde until the intercom on the desk interrupted repeatedly buzzing. The drinking of the wine, the holding of hands and the intimate laughter – the mood was all set until the damn intercom buzzed rudely.

"Mr. President. I'm sorry to disturb you," it was his secretary Laura Henderson's voice. "But it is Mr. Doonan and he says it is urgent."

Roland put down his glass of merlot to push the intercom button. "I'm in the middle of a very important meeting. Can't it wait?"

"This sounds serious," Rebecca said re-buttoning her tight-fitting blouse. "We can wait to do this some other time. As they say all good things come to those who wait."

He kissed the nape of her neck. "I'm not very good at waiting," he said as he started unzipping the back of her skirt.

The intercom buzzed again. "Mr. Doonan says it can't wait."

"Okay," the President said releasing the button. "Give me a few moments."

"Okay, honey bunny," she giggled as she rezipped up skirt and picked up her leather briefcase. She gave his crotch a quick squeeze and then bounced across the lush white carpet of his office floor. She blew Roland a kiss before leaving.

Bannister sighed loudly as he entered, stepped aside for the buxom blonde and stared after her for a moment, he nodded, "Good afternoon Ms. Morton."

Doonan with his arm crossed at the door and waited until the

Marketing Director to be out of earshot. "You must be more careful, Roland. The Board of Trustees won't tolerate a sexual harassment suit."

Bannister sighed. "What is it this time, Paul?" he asked as he pointed to an uncomfortable white chair in front of the massive oak desk. The entire office was decorated in white, but he made sure the chairs his visitors used were always very uncomfortable. It seemed to make meetings much shorter.

Doonan was clearly much older than his boss and shorter, stockier, and much less hair. The Vice President of Enrollment, Communication and Planning pushed his glasses back up onto the bridge of his nose and fumbled with the manila files in his lap.

"I have students showing up asking where they are supposed to be staying for the next few weeks and nobody knows anything about it. I assume these are extras for that movie you agreed to be shot here?"

Bannister nodded.

"Ah, yes. Please take care of that. We have plenty of empty dorm rooms. The crew is supposed to supply their own food and drink and will have their own trailers as well. But I completely forgot about all the extras. But I am sure you can handle it. Can't you?"

Bannister's eyes bore down on his vice president. Those eyes made him seem much more powerful than his frail body conveyed. But in every other way, he was commanding in every sense of the word. Doonan was not exactly afraid of him, but he had felt for years that the man was a little off kilter. But then, weren't most men who considered themselves kings of their kingdoms slightly mad?

"Yes, sir, I will take care of it. And I received the advance check from Terronez Pictures this morning. I will see that it is deposited in the University bank account first thing in the morning."

"I need you to deposit half of that check into the discretionary funds account, Doonan," Bannister told him.

"Sir?"

"Did I stutter, Mr. Doonan?" Bannister asked with a sharp edge in his voice.

"No, sir, but I thought we were using these funds to help

renovate the old Bell Tower. It's really starting to show its age."

"That Bell Tower is the trademark of this school. I don't want anyone touching it. I've already, uh, paid a healthy sum to keep the county from condemning it. Heck, that thing will stand another hundred years. Besides, the money is needed for more important things."

"Sir?"

"They are breaking ground for a new indoor swimming pool and spa beginning tomorrow."

"But, sir, the students already have a pool, and I don't think they need a spa."

"You idiot! Who said the pool was for the students? It's being built on the property the university gave me as part of my renegotiated contract for the coming school year."

"Sir, I... I don't remember the board approving funds for a... a personal swimming pool and spa..."

"You must have missed that meeting, Doonan. But I assure you they approved it. They all seem to love their cushy little jobs as much as you do. Besides, I attend to include a faculty lounge and bar. And we can have some fantastic endowment parties there. So, I see no conflict of interest, do you?"

The Vice President was speechless. He loved this college and had hoped to one day be President. He now realized that there was little hope of that. Bannister's kingdom would stay intact for many years.

"No, sir. Everything seems fine." But in the back of mind, he told himself to remember to make copies of every document passing through this office. Even vultures ended up being meals to other creatures at some point.

***

The hole in the wall in West Hollywood was a seedy strip club called Jugs and was only a few blocks from Santa Monica Boulevard and the Sunset Strip. In its heyday, it had been one of the most popular discos in town. But disco had died long ago, and this sleaze joint was on a respirator and not far away from flat lining as well.

If it were at all possible, the patrons were even sleazier than the dancers. The stripper currently on stage was known as Barbie Doll although she was a freaky clone of the real thing. With silicon breasts that looked anything but natural and lips so injected with collagen that she could barely breathe, she seemed to hang onto the stripper's pole with every ounce of strength left in her aging body.

Donald Becker sat in a far corner of the dark, smoky room. He nursed his watered-down drink and tried to ignore a sixty-year-old lady asking if he wanted a lap dance. She reminded him of his grandmother. He shuddered at the image and pushed her away.

The door opened and Becker recognized the pint-sized reporter, star writer for the Hollywood tabloid *The National Snoop*, walk in and look around. Becker glanced at his watch and signaled the man to his booth.

"You're ten minutes late," Becker said.

"Sorry," the reporter replied. "Someone thought they saw Brad Pitt and Taylor Swift kissing at restaurant on the Westside."

"You're kidding."

"It was a false alarm; it was just some impersonators. But you never know about these things."

"I couldn't care less if you saw Marilyn Monroe walking topless down Colorado Boulevard. I'm paying you good money and don't need you wasting my time."

"Maybe it's not enough," Dane said, testing the waters.

"Just because I fix the teeth for half of Hollywood doesn't mean I'm going to let you rip me off. If you value smiling again, I suggest you don't yank my chain," he said grabbing the little guy by his collar.

"Hey, it's cool."

Becker let go of Dane, then slid an envelope with the second half of the payment across the table. The reporter counted the hundred-dollar bills and smiled.

"What? You don't trust me?" Becker asked.

"Hey. This is Hollywood. I don't trust my own mother."

The diminutive reporter put the envelope in his pocket. "Tough break about you and your, uh, girlfriends. I recently broke up with mine too. Of course, she'll tell the story the other way around. Heartbreak is such..."

"Yeah, yeah, yeah," the dentist said wiping his mouth as he

finished off what might have been the worst tasting beer he'd ever encountered. "Like I give a flying leap. I only want to know what you found out about Desiree Starr." "She's already left town--" Dane replied and then paused as his eyes focused 0n the plump stripper now taking the stage. Becker sighed and nudged him on the arm.

"Oh, sorry," the reporter continued. "She's signed a contract for a zombie movie that's shooting in Florida. *College of the Living Dead* I think it's called. Some little town in Angel Falls. Guess there's some university there or something."

"Never heard of it."

"Me either. It's just a blimp between Tallahassee and Daytona Beach. Guess it was a real tourist stop in the '70s with its Seaside Slide amusement park, but since that place closed, the town's really nowheresville these days. The only thing going for it is Angel Falls University."

"When does shooting start?"

"Right away from what I gather. She visited her parents for a day or two and then headed straight for Angel Falls. Would you like me to keep tabs on her? *The National Snoop* wants me to feed them stories and keep an eye on Geoffrey Terronez. He's under investigation from the FBI for some co-workers he worked with who mysteriously disappeared. It could be a big story if the Feds end up arresting him during filming."

"Not necessary," Becker said as he stood up and threw a twenty-dollar bill on the table as a tip. "It's already taken care of. Maybe I'll see you there. At times like these, I try to follow my code. WWTCD."

"Don't you mean WWJD?"

"No, idiot. WWTCD. 'What Would Tom Cruise Do?' And the answer is: win back the woman. He always gets the chick by the end of the flick." Becker flashed his bright smile and left the joint without another look back.

If he had, he would have seen Dane pocket the twenty-dollar bill he had left as a tip.

"Evil lurks in the minds of men.
We've heard those words again and again.
Yes, Evil whispers in our ears,
And shows us all our deepest fears.
Lurking deep, it sits and waits.
It knows our lust, it knows our fates.
Still we dismiss the words again,
So Evil smiles and walks right in."
-Stan Swanson

V

Zyana
(Part One)
The Escape

"Traitor!"

Zyana hissed the words beneath her breath as her brother stood on the upper level of the Templo Mayor and spoke to the people below in the streets of Tenochtitlan.

"How can my brother say those things?" Zyana asked the old man standing at her side. The man was easily in his sixties, much older than most Aztec people lived. His garb distinguished him as a high priest.

"You know that his words come from fear, my child. He may have driven Cortez and his army from Tenochtitlan once before, but it is unlikely he will be able to do so again. The city will fall this day. Tezcatlipoca has told me so in my dreams. Also, Cihuāpilla Zyana, you should not refer to King Moctezuma as your brother. Unless you want to be offered up as his next sacrifice. While it is true you have the same blood as his father, your mother was a lowly servant who served only to satiate man's earthly desires."

Zyana spit to show her contempt.

"Moctezuma is nothing but a traitor and a coward. His limbs should be tied to four royal steeds and torn apart, then spread like offal in their manure."

The priest laughed. "Ah, yes. Now I see the true spirit of sibling love revealed."

Zyana jerked her head in his direction, her long raven-black hair held in place by a golden headband encrusted with priceless jewels.

"You dare mock me?" she asked, venom in her voice. "Perhaps it is your head we should use as a ball in the next game of Ullamaliztli."

Noctalyc smiled.

Zyana had threatened the elderly priest for years and had never shown him the reverence which would normally be shown a religious leader. The other priests questioned the wisdom of allowing her this "freedom", but he loved her like a daughter. He would be loyal to her until he no longer existed on this earthly plain. Zyana's father had died in battle while she was still a young child and Noctalyc had been by her side ever since.

She still believed that she had a claim to the royal throne. She was not deterred from the fact that Aztec women, although equal to men in some respects, had never ruled and likely never would.

"Instead of preparing for war, my brother speaks of peace and negotiation," she said. "Why would he believe the Spaniards pose no threat even as their army gathers?"

The priest shrugged. "You forget that not long ago your people believed Cortez and the Spaniards to be gods."

"If I were Queen I would drive them from our lands forever," she hissed. "The Aztec bow before no man. But I believe you are correct. The city will fall this day and King Moctezuma will rule no more. And if the city falls, I hope his body rots in the streets."

Her voice trailed off. "If I were Queen . . ." And she said no more.

"It is not to be, my daughter. At least not now. But I have knowledge to share with you when the time is right. For now, we must escape the city while there is still time. The Spaniards march and we do not want to be sealed off. We must retreat to fight another day. The Aztec will need a powerful leader in the future. But the gods have told me this cannot happen until the fields have withered and the city rises once again from the ashes."

"And I will lead them?" Zyana asked, her tone now softer.

"That I do not know," Noctalyc replied truthfully. "I only converse with the gods when they wish it to be so."

"I will not cry for my brother," she said. "But I will shed tears for the city."

"We must go, Zyana," the priest urged. "My body maybe old, but I would rather see my head still attached to my body when the morning sun shows its face tomorrow."

Zyana sighed. "Very well," she replied. "How many go with us?"

"Twenty-four acolytes and twelve slaves. We will take with us as much treasure and gold as we can carry if we are to survive."

They were miles into the jungle when they saw the first plumes of smoke rise from the great city of Tenochtitlan. And Zyana cried in silence.

But it would be the last time she ever showed any sign of weakness.

Part Two

Evil Murmurs

"Strange Ways

You got me in a haze
It's not too promising
To be seen
Seen with you"
-Linnea Quigley

VI

The Swimming Pool

Desiree couldn't sleep. Although she was dead tired, the last few days had been a whirlwind of dramatic events and emotions. But she had to admit her room on the campus of Angel Falls was nice.

She had expected to end up in one of the usual trailers provided for actors while on set, but the producers and directors and several of the leading roles were enjoying the comforts of the House on the Hill.

It would have been comfortable if it hadn't been so hot. She was used to the warmth of California, but the Florida humidity made its presence felt.

And, of course, Gina's snoring didn't help the situation.

She didn't know how her friend slept so peacefully in the other bed. They had agreed to share the two-person room and now Desiree lay wide awake staring at the ceiling with her Victoria's Secret nightshirt clinging to her body from the sweat. She rolled out of bed to splash some water on her face.

Perfect shot for the cameras, she thought to herself as she caught her image in the mirror. The outfit was so soaked it was practically transparent.

The golden orange moon of the night was giving way to the early morning sun and Desiree stepped out onto the small balcony. She had been told by some college official (she thought his name was Dolan or Doonan or something like that) that the House on the Hill was on area of campus known as The Commons that also consisted of the old Bell Tower and Founder's Hall --all that remained of the original Spanish mission and surrounding village. The House on the Hill and Founder's Hall had been thoroughly renovated, but the Bell Tower stood just as it had over two hundred years ago. It was a majestic sight, but Desiree thought it looked like it might topple over if a strong breeze came up.

There were a dozen other newer buildings scattered about the campus, but Desiree hadn't been here long enough to familiarize herself with them. But she already loved the campus which had been designed to maintain the Spanish influence of the original buildings.

She had hoped that by stepping out onto the balcony that she would find a morning breeze to help cool her off, but it didn't happen. But the view from the third story window was spectacular and the water exploding from the fountain in the courtyard very inviting. She knew that the room had air conditioning as it had been going full blast when they had arrived, but sometime during the night it had ceased to work.

She walked back inside and closed the balcony doors behind her. Gina was still snoring away, and Desiree almost felt like waking her up so they could suffer the heat together. Instead, she picked up the phone on the desk and dialed zero with the hope that someone would answer.

She waited patiently as the automated answering system went through a lengthy menu and finally decided she wanted the campus facilities and maintenance department.

Worried that perhaps no one was on duty because of summer break, she was relieved when someone finally answered.

"Facilities, Mick Collins here."

"Thank goodness," she replied. "I'm staying at the House on the Hill and the air conditioner stopped working in the middle of the night. It's so hot in here, I feel like I'm swimming through a pot of chili."

Mick chuckled. "I'll be right up. What room are you in?"

She told him and thought about jumping into the shower as she figured if he was like typical repairmen that he wouldn't show up for hours. But five minutes later there was a knock on the door.

Desiree was expecting the typical image of a short, bald, overweight guy who revealed way too much of his butt-crack when bending over. She was pleasantly surprised to find that Mick Collins was very different from that image. He seemed very fit and was tall with just a trace of gray at the temples of his curly black hair. His dark eyes lit up when Desiree opened the door. When his eyes took a moment to meet hers, she blushed and grabbed the coverlet from the bed to hide her nearly transparent nightwear.

"Sorry," she stammered. "Between the heat and my girlfriend, well, it's been a long night."

"No need to apologize," he replied. He wore a black jersey with the letters "AFU Facilities" embroidered over the pocket of his tight cotton shirt. His khaki-colored chinos were not exactly loose fitting either and Desiree decided that this was one behind she wouldn't mind seeing bent over.

She opened the door wider and let him enter the room. Then she remembered that Gina slept in the buff and was momentarily stumped as to what she should do. The repairman stood there frozen at the sight of the naked, well-built girl on the bed closest to the door. Gina was oblivious, however, and was still sound asleep and snoring away. Of course, knowing Gina, she probably wouldn't care anyway.

"Jeez," Desiree said as she grabbed the sheet Gina had kicked off during the night and covered her up quickly. "I'm sorry. Like I said, it's been a long night."

"No need to apologize," he said with a smile. "This has been my best morning in months. I see that the air conditioner is a Ziegler 2100 – it shouldn't be too hard to fix."

Desiree smiled as he winked at her and then turned his attention to the air-conditioner. Less than ten minutes later the unit was blasting cold air into the room.

"Thanks," Desiree said with a smile. "I really appreciate it, Mr. Collins."

"Hey, my friends call me Mick."

"Okay, Mick," Desiree replied, taking the bait without hesitation.

"Now I know this sounds like a pick-up line, but haven't I seen you somewhere before?"

"Do you like horror films?"

"Sure. Who doesn't except maybe my eighty-year-old grandmother?" He paused then slapped a hand against his forehead. "Jeez. You're Desiree Starr, aren't you. I've seen a ton of your films. I really liked *Hell's Belles, Vampire Vixens from Outer Space, Count Dracula and His Satanic Sluts* and -- that haunted house one."

"Ghost-House III: No Rest for The Wicked."

"How could I forget that one when you ran around in just your panties for half the film. Oh, man, I hope I didn't offend you by saying that."

"No offense," Desiree said with a smile. "I hear it a lot."

"I take it you're here for that new horror flick they're shooting at the university. I thought you had gone mainstream."

"For about a day or two," she replied. "It's a long story. Maybe I can share it with you sometime. But you should know up front that I'm not the type of girl who breaks up marriages."

"What?"

"The faded tan line on your ring finger, Mick. It's a dead giveaway. Did you accidentally lose it at the local strip club?"

He laughed. "Well, first, there's not a strip club within fifty miles of here. And second, my divorce was finalized just two months ago."

"Then maybe I can share that long story with you after all. Here's my business card, Mick. And that's my private cell number. I'll tell you my story and you can tell me yours."

He took the card and placed it in his shirt pocket. He took out a business card and scribbled a phone number on the back.

"This is my card, my cell numbers on the flipside. Ms. Starr, er, Desiree. I'll do that. But guess I'd better get back to work now. I have several more work orders to complete today. Gotta pay for my Viper. It's the only thing I got to keep once the divorce was complete."

"Sweet. You'll have to give me a ride sometime..."

***

Roland Bannister figured that an early morning start might provide relief from the summer Florida heat, but he should have known better. Not that he cared about the workers his brother Randy had dug up from who-knows-where. But it didn't matter if

40

things were kept out of the books for the most part. He'd received a big chunk of money from the film company but didn't plan to waste a cent of it. And, if there was anything left, his house could use a Jacuzzi. Sure, he'd have to pay his brother a hefty amount for this new project, but it was a lot cheaper than hiring real labor. Besides, it was better to keep the money in the family.

He sipped his glass of wine while standing in the shade of an old live oak covered in Spanish moss. He could almost picture himself sitting on the shady veranda of an old southern colonial mansion sipping lemonade while being fanned by a half-naked maid.

The digging for the pool had started at the break of dawn and was moving along swiftly. Two Bobcats were scooping away at the mossy dirt and dumping it in the back of a rented dump track.

But Roland soon became bored as he watched his brother yelling at the workers and keeping them in line. Maybe it's Rebecca Time, he thought although he wouldn't mind a little alone time with that Desiree Starr either. Maybe he could simply think about the Scream Queen while "entertaining" his director of marketing.

He pushed up the front of his expensive Panama hat and wiped the sweat from his brow with his white linen handkerchief. He waved at Randy to signal his brother that he was leaving and turned to walk back towards the main campus when a loud scrapping sound echoed from where one of the Bobcats was working.

Work ground quickly to a halt. Roland pictured his marketing director naked on his desk and briefly debated ignoring the incident when his brother shouted up to him. Roland sighed and made his way through the loose soil and wished he hadn't worn his crocodile-skin shoes.

"What is it?" he asked his brother. "We didn't hit a sewer line, or anything did we? I asked you to make sure to check all of that."

"I did," the younger Bannister said. "There ain't nothing under here unless it's been there a couple of hundred years. Maybe part of the old mission foundation or something. I'll have the guys hook up a chain and yank the thing out in no time."

"No," Roland said putting a hand on his brother's arm. "You never know. If it's something old, it could be valuable. Have the guys dig it out with shovels or something?"

41

Randy nodded and gestured to three of his men.

Twenty minutes later they were digging around the edges of what looked like a giant stone box. Roland gestured for the men to stop and stepped down to the object, no longer concerned with his expensive shoes.

Using his handkerchief, he began wiping away the dirt, muck and mud that covered the box. His heart began beating faster when he revealed some images carved into the stone and he forgot all about seeing Rebecca Morton naked or even Desiree Starr for that matter.

He removed more dirt embedded into the carved relief and the images of naked men and women became clear along with strange signs and drawings he didn't understand the meaning of. On the very top of the stone box was carved the word "Zyanya".

"Anyone know what Zyanya means? Must be Spanish."

"It's not Spanish," one of the workers said.

Randy began helping him clean off the object which they soon discovered was wrapped in chains with old rusty padlocks holding them in place.

"Maybe it's buried Spanish treasure," Randy said, his eyes widening with the prospect. "There could be a fortune of gold and silver and jewels in that thing. Why else would it have chains all around it."

"I don't know," Roland told his brother. "It almost looks like some kind of sarcophagus."

"An esophagus?" the younger brother asked. "Isn't that what you breathe through or leads to your stomach or something?"

"No, you idiot, a sarcophagus," Roland said. "You know, a coffin."

"Un atuád?" one of the workers muttered as he crossed his heart. "Madre de Dios!" The three immigrant workers backed away.

"Great," Roland mumbled. "Now we have a superstitious work crew."

He turned to the trio of workers. "No, no," he said. "No muertas here. No problemo." He hoped they understood as he had just about used up all of the Spanish he had learned in high school.

He let out a long breath and turned to his brother.

"Offer them double time or even triple time, if necessary," he told his brother. "But I want that thing hauled to the storage area of the Ziegler Science Building and locked up tight until Dr. Franklin returns from his trip to the Amazon."

"Triple time?" his brother inquired.

"I said to offer them triple time. I didn't say we were going to pay them. What are they going to do? Run off and report it to the authorities? I highly doubt it since none of them are here legally."

His brother laughed. "Got ya."

Roland nodded and walked off toward the main campus to change clothes. Maybe he'd wait until Dr. Franklin returned and maybe he wouldn't. But regardless, he wasn't going to share whatever was in that box with anyone. Not even his brother.

***

It was late in the day by the time the workers had helped transport the heavy stone container to the science building in the back of his Ford truck. Randy told them to go home for the day but to be back bright and early to continue the construction of the pool. He glanced around and began examining the box. His brother would be crazy to wait until that professor, or whatever he was, come back. Besides, why should he share whatever was in that box with anyone. Even his brother. After all, Randy thought, I'm the one who found it.

He dug a crowbar and flashlight out of the toolbox in the bed of his Ford F-150 and got to work. He tried to labor as quietly as possible as the night air carried sound way too easily on the nearly deserted campus.

But it didn't take long to bust open the rusty padlocks and pull the chains from around the container. All he could envision was a mountain of treasure as he pried open the heavy stone lid. It took every ounce of strength he had, but he cracked open the lid from the box inch by inch, careful not to push it so far that it dropped off to the floor.

He dusted off his hands and grabbed the edge of the box to peer inside, his flashlight blazing. But he didn't find a mound of gold and jewels. It was a body! Randy nearly jumped out of his skin. His brother had been right. It was a coffin. The strange thing was that the body inside seemed perfectly preserved. It was a

43

woman, tall and dark with raven-black hair. And she was naked. It looked like her clothing had simply turned to dust years ago and now the slight evening breeze wisped away the final remnants of dust.

He admired the perfect form of the body from the long muscular legs to the well-proportioned breasts. But his eyes finally came to rest on the diamond and emerald encrusted necklace lying between those magnificent mounds.

Randy laughed. That pair of melons would do any Hooters waitress or female weatherwoman with names like Windy, Stormy or Sunny proud, he thought.

But strangely enough for a womanizer like Randy, his eyes drifted back to the jeweled necklace that sparkled in the glow of his flashlight. The woman also wore matching earrings and an intricate gold headdress formed into the shape of a snake.

Randy reached for the necklace but froze when a cold hand was wrapped around his arm. He gasped and tried to jerk his arm free, but her grip was as strong as a vise. His heart skipped a beat as he watched her eyelids open, and the irises of her eyes change from ebony to a crimson red that nearly matched her lips. And when those lips parted, he couldn't take his eyes off the very white and very sharp fangs.

And Randy no longer cared whether anyone heard anything or not. His initial scream was one of fear. His last was one of intense pain.

"Cast and crew
Fueled by brew
Waiting for the picture to begin
Lights! Cameras! Zombie extra take-off your top"
-Michael McCarty

VII

Topless Zombie Pool Party

Desiree was in the shower when she heard the familiar ring of her cell phone. She briefly thought about ignoring it. The tender sting of the shower felt wonderful after a restless night, but when the phone kept ringing, she sighed. She turned off the water, grabbed a towel from the rack and wrapped it around her. The blast of the repaired air conditioner washed over her, and she felt a wave of goose bumps cover her bare skin. She shivered, but it refreshed her. It was almost too cold now and felt like a meat locker instead of the microwave oven heat of earlier. She thought about turning the thermostat down a bit, but was afraid it she touched it, it might stop working again.

She recognized the voice immediately. It was Geoffrey Terronez. "Hey, Des," he said. "Just checking in and seeing how you like your accommodations and to let you know I'm staying at the Motel 99 here in Angel Falls."

"I thought you were staying here on campus, Geoffrey? They have some nice dorm rooms here at the House on the Hill. Must be reserved for seniors or something."

"It's a long story," he said. "I figured with you, Gina and Lu all staying there it would sort of become No-Man's-Land. But this place is great, and I got a great rate because they think I'm some hot shot movie director."

"You are a hotshot movie director," Desiree insisted.

Terronez chucked. "Well, filming doesn't start until tomorrow, but this could be my biggest film ever. It's got a great script and a beautiful lead actress."

If the director had been in the room, he would have seen Desiree blush.

"Anyway," he said. "I know I'll see everyone on the set tomorrow, but I've decided to give a pool party here tonight to get things rolling and let everyone get loose. This motel is dead because it's a college town in the middle of summer and they have a sweet pool area. So, I've decided it's time for a topless zombie pool party, my love."

"Topless?" Desiree chuckled. "How surprising."

He laughed. "Well, it's not mandatory. Except for some of the extras who are playing the roles of the undead. I need to test out the make-up and make sure it's waterproof. We'll also have plenty of food, booze and a band. Well, if you can call Sewer Rat and the two old rockers, he found on the beach yesterday a band. It will be a great chance for everyone to mingle before production starts. I figure the soiree will kick off about ten."

"Do I have to attend?" Desiree asked. "I didn't sleep that great last night because the air conditioner conked out."

"What do you think?" was his answer and she could tell he really required no answer.

"Fine. I'll be there with bells on. And, just so you know, a swimming suit top too."

He laughed again and hung up.

"Crap," the Scream Queen said to herself. She hated these things and certainly didn't want to go by herself, she sat on the bed for a few moments as she absent-mindedly dried her hair. She finally opened her purse and found the business card she was looking for.

She hesitated, then dialed the number. She wasn't sure if she wanted him to answer or not. When he did, she became less nervous and was glad she had dialed.

"Mick Collins at your service."

"Hey, Mick," she said. "They're throwing a pre-production party tonight for the movie and I really don't feel like going alone. You want to hang out a pool with a bunch of topless zombies?"

He never hesitated. "How can I pass up an offer like that?"

"Can't resist staring at a bunch of girls with their boobs hanging out, huh?"

"Hey," he replied. "Who's going to be staring at naked girls when I have a date as beautiful as you."

It was the second time within just a few minutes that Desiree blushed.

***

Greg Dane stood on the third-floor balcony in front of his room and smiled.

The cast party was pretty much in full swing. And, although the band was bad, alcohol made them seem much better than they were. He was enjoying watching the zombie extras (he was always a sucker for a good zombie movie), but even more so, he was enjoying a dozen bare breasts as well.

Terronez must have requested that most of the lights be turned off to enhance the tiki torches surrounding the pool. Luckily for him, most of the rooms were either empty or occupied by people associated with the movie. The request had apparently been requested.

He heard footsteps in the darkness, and it caught him off guard. He figured everyone would be down at the pool. He whirled around quickly. After seeing the "zombies" in the pool below, his heart skipped a beat. That was the problem when you were a horror movie fan. There always seemed to be creatures coming out of the darkness.

He made out a tall dark figure in the shadows.

"All alone?" came a deep voice.

Dane squinted, then smiled. "Hey, it's Mr. Clean."

Zach Wawrzyniak stepped forward and held out his hand. They shook and then both leaned forward against the railing to enjoy the view below.

"I haven't been called Mr. Clean in ages, Shorty."

"Touché," Greg replied. "But then again, you haven't had hair in ages."

"Ouch, now that hurts."

"I didn't expect you to be here," Greg said, and you could hear the disappointment in his voice. Reporters were usually friendly with each other (especially after a couple of beers), but things changed if they ended up working the same story.

"Don't get your boxers in a twist. We are, after all, two brothers of the media."

"I can't believe that *Monster Agogo Magazine* sent you here to do some fluff piece."

Zach opened the can of beer he had carried up from the pool party. "Ouch, that hurts even more, but I suppose I had that one coming. You've probably heard that *MAM is* going down the crapper. We probably only have a couple of issues left before the print version folds. The online magazine is doing okay. They have a hell of a lot of free subscribers, but not many paid advertisers yet. I've come down here to see if I can do a freelance story or two. Do you know if *The National Snoop* might be interested in anything? I have some interesting leads."

"Maybe. But you're gonna must supply me with booze for the rest of the time we're here and don't step on any of my own leads. I'll be seeing my editor, Ed Devin, in the morning and give you a good word, but everything should be copasetic. Deal?"

He held his hand out to shake to seal the agreement.

"Deal," Zach said as he grasped Greg's hand. "Except everything's up for grabs when it comes to Geoffrey Terronez. Okay?"

Greg shrugged. "I guess so. Do you think he really did any of the stuff he's being accused of?"

"Hey, where there's smoke, there's fire. And I think there's a huge blaze surrounding that guy. I love his special effects. He's a genius, but you gotta admit the guy's a little creepy."

"So, shall we join the zombies down below?"

"You bet," Zach replied. "I might even accidentally bump into a boob or two before the evening is over."

The two men laughed and headed downstairs.

They failed to notice a third figure standing in the shadows.

***

Mick pulled up to the front of the House on the Hill driving his black Dodge Viper convertible which was as slick as the night. Desiree laughed when he stepped from the car bare-chested.

"Hey," he said as he posed like someone on the cover of *Men's Sports* magazine. "You said it was a topless party."

Desiree smiled as he opened the passenger door for her and tried not to be obvious as she admired his bare chest. She wore the same black and white stripped bikini that had caused her boy-toy dentist to drool just a few days earlier. It was covered by a very transparent swim cover-up and was having the same effect on the facilities man too. She was pleasantly surprised that she was finding it easier and easier to put Donald Becker in the past.

It only took them a couple of minutes to reach Motel 99 and they found the party already in high gear. The scene looked like a cross between a George Romero zombie movie and a strip club. In the center of it all sat Geoffrey Terronez wearing white PJs, dark sunglasses, and a gold-colored crown that Desiree figured was probably made of plastic or painted tin, but with Terronez, you never knew.

"Welcome to the Tragic Kingdom," the director said with a slight slur and an almost empty Margarita glass in his hand. "Milk-Maiden Starr, who might be this knave you bring to my court?"

"Hello, Geoffrey. I'd like you to meet Mick Collins. He works here at the college." She failed to mention that on her date worked in the maintenance department. The director tended to judge people much too often by what they did for a living. "Mick, this the director Geoffrey Terronez."

"Make that Sir Geoffrey," Terronez corrected. "The Lord of Gore at your service."

"I thought your official title was the Wizard of Ooze," Desiree teased.

Terronez removed his fake crown, fumbled at the table near his chair and replaced the crown with a pointy wizard cap that looked like it had been purchased at The Wizarding World of Harry Potter in Orlando. "I have lots of hats," he said, "and lots of nicknames, but only one head. Well, two actually, but we won't discuss that in mixed company."

This caused Desiree and Mick to grin.

"Booze is over there," Geoffrey pointed off to his left. "And the food is right beside it. Any questions?"

"Have you seen Gina Bellarossi?" Desiree asked. "I haven't seen her since this morning."

"Hmmm..," the director mused as he scratched his goatee. "I believe I saw her headed towards room 2B." He laughed and shifted to his best British accent which wasn't too good after several Margaritas. "2B or not 2B, that is the question."

"Thanks," Desiree said as she took her date's hand. "I want to introduce her to Mick."

Terronez waved them away as if were dismissing them from his court, and suddenly noticed a dark-haired buxom lady sans her top and wearing only a thin thong that barely concealed anything.

"Oh, my," Geoffrey said as he reached out and took the lady's hand. He kissed it and then didn't release his grip. "Welcome to my Kingdom. Are you one of my handmaidens?"

She smiled slyly. "Maybe that and more, Mr. Terronez," she said. "I've been and admirer of your work for years."

"Well, I know you're not an extra, because I scoured all the strip clubs in the area to cast them myself. Not that I'm comparing you to a stripper," he told her. "Although I must admit you have the correct attributes."

She laughed. "I'm Rebecca Morton, the university's Director of Marketing. Guess you could say I'm sort of crashing your party. But it gets boring around here in the summer and it's just nice to kick back a little, if you know what I mean."

"Crash all ye like, my lady. You have me under your magical powers."

"Well, I don't have any magical powers, except occasional raising revenue for FAU," she replied with a wink. "Do you have any special powers?"

"Ohhhhh, yes," Geoffrey said. "Come back to my room, er, I mean my suite and I'll show you. I might even let you rub my magic Genie lamp and see if we can make both of our wishes come true."

She laughed and followed him across the courtyard to his room.

This summer is going to be more exciting than I thought, she said to herself.

***

The door to 2B was wide open, so Desiree and Mick walked in. Terronez had stored much of his editing and monitoring equipment and although the room was crammed with cameras, computers and monitors, there was still plenty of room for a sofa, two huge easy chairs and a coffee table.

Gina was on the sofa laughing with a hot young Latino beauty that Desiree did not recognize. Michelangelo lounged in one of the easy chairs with his girlfriend, PJ Bottoms, sitting on his lap, nibbling at his ear. Both had major roles in the upcoming film.

Gina waved briefly, but Desiree could tell she was making a play for the beauty sitting on the sofa beside her.

PJ looked up and displayed a plastic smile. "My, my, if it isn't Desiree Starr and, well, who's this? Your newest boy-toy? Except he is much older than your usual taste in men."

Desiree felt like smacking her across the face, but instead she simply said, "Mick, this is PJ and Michelangelo. PJ, I'm surprised you still have your top on. Or your bottom for that matter."

Michelangelo interrupted the conversation before things got out of hand between Desiree and his girlfriend. "There's beer in the bathtub. We filled it ice to keep it cold. Got tired of running out to the pool and grabbing more when we needed one. Plus, Sewer Rat's music is just too loud. If you can even call it music."

PJ got up. "Well, no one thought about food. I'm hungry. I'm gonna go grab some of those snacks out there and bring them in."

She gave Desiree a dirty look as she walked past and out the door.

Gina waved them over, barely able to tear her eyes away from her enticing female companion. "Hey, Des, this is Rio Ruiz. She's a big name in Brazil, but she wants to break into American films, so she signed on as an extra to get her foot in the door."

"Hola," Rio said with a broad smile revealing teeth Donald Becker would have approved of.

Gina nodded at Mick. "So, who's your handsome companion?"

Desiree went through introductions for the third time that evening.

"Glad to make your acquaintance, Mick," Gina said.

"Actually, er, we kinda met," Mick said turning slightly red in the face.

"We did?" Gina commented as her eyebrows curled up. "I don't think I could have forgotten you. I might like girls, but I know a hunk when I see one."

"I work for the facilities department at the college. I worked on your air conditioner this morning."

"Oh," she said, remembering she slept sans clothing. She smiled sheepishly and shrugged. "Cie la vie. You guys want a beer? I'll go get one."

"Sounds good to me," Mick said and tried not to follow Gina's rear end as she left the room.

Desiree nudged him. "I'll forgive you this one time," she whispered.

He grinned. "Sorry. So, tell me so I can catch up on all the Hollywood gossip. And I don't mean this the wrong way. Just curious. Have you ever slept with Geoffrey Terronez?"

"Heaven's no," Desiree said, slightly shocked at the question. "I don't sleep with directors. They must tell you every move to make while filming, I wouldn't want them to tell me every move to make in bed too. Anyway, he's totally not my type. He's too skinny. You'd have to shake the sheets to find him."

"Well, if you want some gossip, I saw that PJ chick flirting with him earlier today. Wouldn't be surprised if she was doing a little sheet-shaking."

"PJ?" Desiree thought about it. "Wouldn't surprise me. She'd do just about anything to get future roles, but I think she's pretty much head over heels for Michelangelo. They've been together for quite a while."

"Well, don't look now, but I don't think he feels the same way."

"What?" Desiree inquired.

Mick pointed to the couch where PJ's boyfriend was now snuggling with the Brazilian beauty. He whispered something in her ear, and she laughed as his hand settled on her thigh and slid slowly upward. Rio seemed like she was about to object when PJ walked back into the room.

She dropped the tray full of food she was carrying, and sandwiches and chips scattered over the carpet. She started to say something as Michelangelo leaped up to explain the situation, but she ran from the room before he had a chance to say a word.

Desiree couldn't help but smile. "Jeez, I didn't really want to come to this thing, but this evening is looking more exciting all the time."

***

PJ Bottoms ran in the general direction of the campus but lost her way in the wooded area between the town and the university.

She heard something off to her left and stopped running, trying to catch her breath.

"You son-of-a-bitch!" she screamed. "How could you? I thought you loved me!"

At first, she thought the hand on her wrist belonged to Michelangelo and she tried to jerk it away. It didn't work and in fact, she was shoved roughly to the ground.

"What the hell are you—?"

It was her last words. Soft lips lovingly touched her throat, but then sharp fangs sunk into her neck. She gasped, but quickly lost consciousness as the warm blood flowed from the open wound and into a welcoming mouth.

"Strange ways
You got me in a rage
It's not too promising
To be seen
Seen with you"
-Linnea Quigley

VIII

Breakfast of the
Living Dead

Gina Bellarossi sat in the dining room on the lower level of the East End Dorms and sipped at her coffee. It was hot, humid, and hazy and much too early to be up (especially after partying half the night), but she hadn't been able to sleep either. It was always that way with her on the first day of filming.

The food that was being catered in by the Golden Gator, one of Angel Falls few restaurants, smelled delicious, but she also didn't eat much on the first day of filming. Although she had been in dozens of films, she always felt nauseous on the first day. She sure didn't want to be barfing in her first scene.

Most of the cast and crew were there except for Geoffrey Terronez, PJ Bottoms and Desiree Starr. Rumors of a ménage trio were being discussed in whispers at the table next to her, but she knew Desiree didn't sleep with directors. In fact, her friend was very picky when it came to choosing her bedmates.

Gina was also a little disappointed not to have gotten to know Rio Ruiz a little better. But that feeling faded somewhat when one of the big-breasted zombie extras walked up to her table. She had noticed early in her career that the lower the budget of the film, the bigger the cup size. Of course, in the case of Geoffrey Terronez, the ability to fill out a bikini top was always a top priority.

The tall blonde juggled a huge tray filled with pancakes, eggs, bacon and grits. Either it was too early in her career to worry about her figure, or her metabolism was the envy of every starlet in Hollywood. She still wore her zombie make-up from the previous evening.

The girl smiled. "Hi, I'm Barbara. Mind if I join you?"

"Certainly," Gina replied, hoping the girl's boobs might simply fall out of her flimsy, torn top.

The girl sat down. "Sorry about the make-up. Mr. Terronez really wants to see how long it will hold up. I don't think I even have a scene until tomorrow."

"No problem," Gina replied as she held out her hand. "I've been in more than one of these things."

"Oh, my God," the buxom girl gushed. "You're Gina Bellarossi, aren't you? I thought it was you. Can we get our picture taken together some time?"

Gina smiled. "Oh, my dear, I am sure that can be arranged."

"I loved you in *Neanderthal Nurses from the Northlands*. And your performance in *Blood Brothel Mama* was incredible."

"Thank you," Gina said. "Both films were fun to do, but I was a little pissed when they cut several of my scenes in BBM."

"Well, then, the film editors were idiots. You were fabulous in what scenes survived on the screen."

"Thanks," Gina replied. "It's always nice—"

Half of the blonde's rotted face suddenly plopped down into the syrupy center of her pancakes.

"Well, that's not good," she said, and Gina couldn't tell if she was more disappointed with her makeup or having her breakfast ruined. "I guess I'd better check in with Lucretia. Sorry to rush off."

"Oh, I'm sure we'll see much more of each other," Gina assured her and watched the girl's firm backside as she left the dining hall.

Gina signed. She glanced at her watch and decided to check in with PJ. They were both in a very early scene. PJs phone rang and then went to a recorded message. She hung up and dialed Desiree who answered on the second ring.

"Where are you?" Gina asked when her fellow Scream Queen answered.

Desiree sounded out of breath and Gina wondered if she had interrupted something. Had that maintenance guy come in after Gina had left their room? She felt her face turn pink and started to apologize when Desiree replied.

"I'm doing some yoga and exercises. I don't like interrupting my daily routine even during filming."

"Have you seen PJ?" Gina asked.

"Sorry," Desiree said. "Haven't seen her since she ran out the door crying last night. You think she's in trouble or something?"

"Nah," Gina said. "She's probably on set already. We have an early scene together."

"I'm going to go down after a quick shower. I don't have a scene until later, but I've always been one of those to hang around no matter what. You'd be amazed what skills you can pick up. Can't be a Scream Queen forever, you know."

"Don't I know it," Gina said. "I'll see you in a few."

***

Desiree had just flipped her phone shut when it rang again. It startled her so much she almost dropped it. She opened it again as she headed for the bathroom to take a shower.

"Ms. Starr? Mick Collins here. I just wanted to check and see if your air conditioner was still working properly."

Desiree laughed. "Why the formal tone, Mick?"

"Well," he said in a hushed voice. "We're really not supposed to make personal calls during working hours."

"So, is this just an excuse to come over to see me?"

"Well, you know. If you're still having problems, I'd sure like to help."

Desiree grinned. "Well, unfortunately I'll be on the set most of the day."

He sounded disappointed. "Oh, okay, Yeah, no problem."

"Now don't be a hurt puppy dog, Mick. I'm not trying to chase you off. I should be done and off the set by around eight tonight. But you know if you're still working or have a date or something..."

It was now his turn to laugh. "Touché."

"I need to get moving, Mick. Got to take a quick shower before I go mingle with the zombies."

"Are you sure your shower is working, okay?" he asked. "I could come check that out."

"Now, Mick. We've only had one date."

"And tonight, will make two," he said. "And you know what they say about the third date."

"Don't get your hopes up, Mr. Collins. I don't always play by the rules. But I'm sure looking forward to a couple of fancy meals and some expensive wine."

"Did you forget we are in Angel Falls?" he asked. "How about a burger and a beer down at Swampy's Tavern. And they serve a mean appetizer of gator too."

Desiree 's mouth went dry, and she couldn't talk for a moment."

"Desiree?"

She took a deep breath. "Sorry, Mick. Just make sure not to order any appetizers, okay? I have a real dislike for gators and anything else that comes out of a swamp and I'm vegan too."

"Damn," he replied. "How could I have forgotten? I'm so sorry. Just wasn't thinking."

She shook off the feeling of dread. "No biggie. See you at eight?"

"Yes, ma'am," he said. "And I'll even wear a shirt this time."

She laughed, feeling much better. "Well, Mick, I don't know if that's a good thing or a bad thing."

***

Roland Bannister tied the shoelaces of his new Nike running shoes and tried to decide where he would do some jogging. Twice a month he started a new exercise routine and it never lasted for more than a couple of days. He was trying to decide whether it was too hot for his $200 jogging jacket when Paul Doonan drove up in one of the campus' golf carts. His face told Bannister that something else was bothering the man. He wondered what it was this time. Maybe he had lost a dollar in the Coke machine. What a loser, he thought. I'd fire him if he didn't know where all my secrets were buried.

"Hello, Paul," Bannister said. "What is the problem now? I

have a busy schedule this morning."

"I just thought you should know that I had a very big and very angry Latino storm into my office looking for you. I think he said his name was Roberto Martinez."

Bannister shrugged. "Never heard of him."

"Apparently, he's one of the crew working on the new pool. He told him and his friends were promised some extra dinero the night before last for moving something over to the science building. He says they never got paid. They refuse to work until they get their money."

"Hell," Bannister said, clearly irritated. "My brother is handling all of that. Go find him. It's not my problem."

"Well, that's the other thing. No one has seen your brother for the past two days."

"Jeez, why am I surrounded by imbeciles? He probably went on a bender again. Go check all the bars and cheap motels in Angel Falls."

"That really isn't my job, Roland," Doonan replied.

Bannister's eyes narrowed. "It's your job if I say it's your job. Got that?"

Doonan bit his lip to keep himself from saying the wrong thing. "Fine, but someone needs to deal with the workers if you want construction to remain on schedule."

"Jesus on a stick," Bannister swore. He took out his wallet and counted the amount of cash he had on hand. "Fine, let's go pay the workers and then you can head into Angel Falls. Hell, I'd fire the son-of-a-bitch if he weren't my brother."

Bannister punched buttons on his cell phone all the way to the work site. His brother's cell phone, work phone and home phone all went directly to voicemail.

They drove to the worksite and Bannister quickly paid off the irate workers, but there was no sign of his brother.

"Drive over to the science building," he told Doonan and a minute later they parked next to a familiar red Ford pickup.

"Well, that's my brother's truck," Bannister said. "It's unlikely he went into town. Maybe he got drunk and hooked up with one of the extras or something."

But then he remembered the stone sarcophagus he had told

Randy and the crew to bring here. His pulse rate increased.

"You got your keys?" he asked Doonan.

The Vice President nodded. "Let's go. I had Randy drop something off for storage and it had damned well still better be here."

The two men entered the science building loading dock.

The sarcophagus was alright there but the locks and chains had been broken off and the stone lid had slid to one side where it balanced precariously.

Bannister swore and then gazed down into the interior of the stone coffin.

There was nothing there but a thick layer of cobwebs and a couple of small red spiders.

"Goddamn it," Roland said as he brought his hand angrily down on the lid. The impact unbalanced the heavy stone and it crashed to the floor and broke into several large pieces.

One of them struck Doonan's foot and he hopped around swearing, but Bannister didn't even notice. "He's taken the treasure..."

Doonan massaged his foot as he spoke. "What treasure? What the hell are you talking about?"

Bannister continued to ignore him and kept muttering to himself, nearly on the edge of losing it. "But why the hell didn't he take his truck?"

Doonan cleared his throat. "I saw Geoffrey Terronez roaming around the whole campus yesterday," he said.

"So? What the hell does that have to do with the price of coffee in China?"

"I think you mean the price of tea in China," Doonan replied.

"What in God's name are you talking about?" Bannister demanded.

"Never mind, but I have no idea what treasure you are talking about, but surely you've heard the rumors about Terronez."

"Doonan, if you don't explain to me in plain English what you're trying to say, I'm going to shove my Nikes so far up your ass you'll see every friggin' Greek goddess there ever was."

"There's been people gone missing on nearly every movie Geoffrey Terronez ever made. The cops even brought him in for questioning last week in L.A."

"Except that doesn't explain my missing treasure," Bannister snapped.

Doonan limped to a railing near the dock and leaned on it for support, his ankle throbbing. "Do you want me to call the authorities?"

"No, no, no!" Bannister yelled as he clutched the side of his head. He could feel a bad migraine coming on. "The publicity could hurt enrollment. Fall registration is just around the corner. And I sure don't want the Board of Trustees or boosters getting wind of this. There must be a logical explanation. In the meantime, have security beef things up 24/7."

Doonan nodded. "I'll call Slim Jim right away."

"Who?"

"Slim Jim Atkins," Doonan replied. "He's head of security. You really should get to know your staff a little better."

Bannister glared at him and grabbed the keys to the golf cart.

"What I'm going to do is go have a nice little talk with this Terronez guy."

Doonan watched his boss hurry down the concrete steps towards the golf cart.

"Roland?" he called as his boss started to drive away. "What about my foot? I can barely walk."

And then all he could do was stand there and watch as Bannister drove away.

***

Roland pushed the golf cart to its top speed limit (which wasn't very fast) driving wildly along some pedestrian paths that were barely wide enough for a single person walking. He knocked at least two sprinkler heads off their mounts and nearly ran over a maintenance man near one of the campus' many fountains.

He reached the East End Dorms and jumped off the golf cart which kept rolling and mowed down a small bed of flowers before it slowed to a halt. Many of the cast members and crew of *College of the Living Dead* were still in the dining hall finishing up breakfast.

Off in one corner, a well-endowed female zombie was having her makeup reapplied by a woman he recognized as Terronez's sister.

He stomped up to her, his face red with rage and exertion.

"Where's your brother," he demanded.

"Last time I saw him he was across the quad in one of the dorm rooms. 13A, I think, although I stopped keeping tabs on my brother years ago. He should be headed to the set shortly—"

Before she could finish her sentence, Bannister pushed his way back out of the dining hall and headed straight for dorm rooms across the campus' quad.

The president of the campus knocked angrily on the door of room 13A until it finally opened. He was speechless for a moment when Rebecca Morton, Angel Fall University's Director of Marketing, answered the door wearing nothing more than a thin blanket she had wrapped around herself.

"Rebecca?" he said in a strangled voice. "What..."

Still groggy, the woman tried to shade her eyes from the early morning sun. At first, she couldn't even tell who was at the door.

Deciding he had bigger problems than whom Rebecca Morton was sleeping with, he regained his composure. "I need to talk to Geoffrey Terronez."

The director apparently heard the request and walked to the door, also draped with a similar blanket. "Yeah?"

"I need to know if you know anything about my brother!" Bannister said, his finger poking straight into Terronez's face.

The director simply yawned and wrapped an arm around Rebecca who was suddenly uncomfortable with the whole situation but didn't know what to do except simply stand there. "Your brother? Hell, I didn't even know you had a brother."

"His name is Randy. He's foreman of the construction crew that does projects for the university."

"Sorry. Never heard of him. If you're asking if he can appear as a zombie extra or something, send him over to see Lu. It's fine with me. Now, I have some business to finish before I head to the set. Have a good day."

And before Bannister could respond, the director slammed the door in his face.

"You son-of-a-bitch!" Bannister shouted. "If you did anything to my brother, you'll pay for it if it's the last thing I do!"

**

61

Geoffrey Terronez and Rebecca had barely finished dressing when there was another knock on the door. The director expected to find the crazy college president standing there, but it was Michelangelo DeSalvo, one of the starring actors.

"Geoffrey," the Italian actor gasped, breathless from his dash from the motel to the campus. "We have a problem."

"We?" Geoffrey said cocking an eyebrow.

"I can't find PJ anywhere. I looked for her for half the night. She's missing."

"Missing?" Terronez threw his hands into the air. "Another missing person?" He was now more concerned as it involved one of his people. He took some deep breaths. "Why would she be missing?"

"Well, I had a little too much to drink last night and she caught me flirting with Rio."

"Rio Ruiz?" the director asked, trying to comprehend everything that had happened in the last few minutes.

Clearly frustrated, Michelangelo clinched his fists at his sides. "Yes! Rio Ruiz. How many Rios do you think we have running around here? I know she was upset with me, but she never returned to our room last night and no one else has seen her."

The director thought about the situation.

"Maybe she just headed back home to L.A."

"I don't think she'd do that. She wouldn't want to jeopardize her part in the movie. Besides, all her clothes are still in our room."

"This is just great!" Terronez threw his arms into the air. "Absolutely frigging great! She has scenes to shoot this morning. Track her down and tell her she's fired if she doesn't get back on set by noon. I guess in the meantime I can shoot the close-ups of Desiree 's with the helicopter and have the stunt doubles do the others."

He dismissed the man with a wave of his hand.

"Actors – I hope my next film is a cartoon," he muttered as he slammed the door shut once again.

"Dark carnival
Carnival at night
No rides or lights
Or clowns to fright"
-Michael McCarty

IX

Dark Carnival

Desiree had never had a more grueling day of filming. The first scene in the script had sounded relatively easy. A few shots of the interior of the Robinson R44 Raven II helicopter, and even fewer lines, sounded like a breeze. It turned into a nightmare. As usual, Geoffrey Terronez was a perfectionist (although Desiree preferred the term anal) and even when a scene seemed fine, they ended up reshooting.

Of course, Desiree knew the director was desperate to get most of the short rental contract for the copter, so breaks were short and few, even in the terrible conditions.

The temperature was in the high 90s, which was closing in on the record for the area, but it was the humidity that made it nearly unbearable. Of course, the enclosed cabin of the copter made things even worse. Desiree figured it must be close to 110 degrees where she sat in the pilot's seat. She chugged bottle after bottle of water to keep from getting dehydrated. Unfortunately, the state-of-the-art aircraft had air conditioning, but it couldn't be turned on. They couldn't power up the whirlybird because the blades would have caused too much noise during filming and turning on the air would only have drained the aircraft's batteries.

Filming took even longer than everyone had counted on simply because they had to call a break every five minutes so makeup could wipe the sweat from her face and reapply her cosmetics. Terronez finally called for a wrap late in the day and

63

Desiree said a silent prayer.

Maybe I'm not getting paid enough, she thought. Much more of this and I'll simply liquefy into a blob of flesh in the pilot's seat.

"About time, Geoffrey," the Scream Queen gasped. "My Spanx are getting swampy."

"Hold on," he said before she could climb down. "Just one more shot, darling."

"Cheese and Crackers, Geoffrey. Come on. I'm melting in here. I feel like I'm a character in the House of Wax and everything's burning around me. And, of course, I refer to the Vincent Price version and not that horrible remake with Paris Hilton."

He laughed. "We just need something for the blooper reel. Make a face or something."

Desiree crossed her eyes and stuck out her tongue.

Before the director even had a chance to yell 'cut,' she was climbing out of the cockpit and grabbed another bottle of Dasani.

"Nice job, Des," Terronez said as the Scream Queen wiped the sweat from her face. "Go grab a shower if you'd like, but I want everyone one in my suite at the motel in one hour, okay? Looks like we already must make some script changes and probably more than that. We're only on the first day of shooting and already behind schedule. Maybe Hell's Belles ended up being a financial success, but it was almost a disaster. I'm not about to go through all that again, so I intend to set things straight right now. If anyone doesn't like it, they can hit the road."

Desiree nodded but didn't ask any questions. But she would have been sweating now even if she had been standing on a glacier in Alaska. When Geoffrey Terronez was upset, someone was going to pay the price.

***

Terronez's suite was crowded and Desiree, although she was ten minutes early, was the last to arrive. The song of the cicadas in the nearby cypress trees was gradually tapering off as evening approached and it disappeared completely when she closed the door behind her.

Geoffrey Terronez stood in his usual spot (no matter where a meeting took place) next to the bar, a drink in his hand. His sister,

Lucreita straightened the hem of her white summer dress as she shifted on one of the room's sofas. Producer Blake Smith sat next to her but seemed bored. He was dressed in Bermuda shorts and a loud lime green shirt. Mr. Twinks, his teddy bear, and constant travelling companion wore the exact same outfit. In miniature, of course.

Desiree nodded a quick 'hello' to Gina who was standing next to Michelangelo DeSalvo. A few other actors and actresses were also present as were the head cameraman and soundman. She didn't even recognize the tall woman seated on a barstool near Terronez. She would find out later that it was Rebecca Morton, the university's Director of Marketing and Geoffrey Terronez's latest conquest.

"Okay," Terronez said as he poured himself another drink. "Let's get things started so everyone can get a good night's rest. This film is going to stay on schedule and on budget, so I'm going to make that clear right now."

Several people in the room shifted uncomfortably in the chairs. Terronez fixed his stare on Michelangelo.

"Now, Mr. DeSalvo, it seems we have a problem. No one seems to be able to find your girlfriend. Where is she?"

"What do you mean we?" Michelangelo scowled. "How the hell should I know where she is?"

"Because you're the one who was flirting with someone else when she ran out the door crying."

"Not my problem," the actor replied. "The bitch can fall into a hole and die for all I care. I've never seen anyone with PMS 365 days a year."

Most of the room gasped and Blake even covered the ears of Mr. Twinks.

Strangely enough, Terronez smiled. "Just the attitude I expected from a half-rate actor. Mr. DeSalvo, you may pack your bags and leave the set. You're fired."

"What? You can't fire me."

"Perhaps you should read your contract a little closer. Pack your bags and get the hell out. You're toast. And you will never work on another film that I am associated with. My office will send your severance check in the mail. I want you gone first thing in the

65

morning. If you are still on campus after that time, I will have you escorted from the college. Do I make myself perfectly clear?"

"Fine," the actor spat. "I'd just like to know why it's always your sets where people end up disappearing, you half-assed prima donna. Don't think everyone here doesn't know that." He headed for the door. "And the rest of you had better watch your backs."

And with that, he slammed the door behind him.

Geoffrey clapped his hands and took a deep breath. "Okay, that went much smoother than I thought. At least I didn't get punched in the face like the last time I fired someone. And that one was a girl." He laughed and his anger seemed gone, but his face was still filled with lines of concern.

"Now I realize most of you are close to PJ and she's a great little actress, but we can't hold up shooting. We must replace her. I thought maybe Lu could take on the role, but her duties as associate producer, makeup and special effects coordinator are already more than I can ask. Plus, she claims her acting days are behind her. I've put in some calls to Hollywood and New York, but no luck so far and I don't know how long I can shoot around her scenes."

"Well, Mr. Terronez," Desiree offered. "I think Gina could take on that part easily. I've worked with her for years. I think she could step in without a hiccup."

The director stroked his goatee and thought for a moment, then nodded. "Great idea, Des. I've seen some of her work and she certainly deserves more than a bit part in *College of the Living Dead*. How about it, Ms. Bellarossi?"

"Are you kidding?" Gina exclaimed as she jumped off the couch and gave the director a big hug. "I won't let you down." Terronez didn't mind the huge squeeze from the big-breasted star a bit, but Rebecca Morton did not seem pleased. She was like a dog who had already placed its mark on its territory.

Gina sat back down and threw Desiree a kiss.

"Well, that solves that, but it does create another problem. We now need someone who can take on Gina's old role. Any suggestions?"

"How about Rio?" Gina suggested, suddenly brave with her newfound role.

But to her disappointment, the director didn't seem impressed. "I think Rio has a bright future here in the States, but she needs to work on her English a lot. We'd have to do too many script changes."

"What about Barbara Quincy?" Lucretia suggested. "She's currently one of the zombie extras."

"Is she the stripper from Reno?" Terronez asked.

Lucretia nodded. "Yes, you always remember the strippers, don't you, dear brother. But I think she's done some community theater too and the part doesn't have that many scenes. Gina and Desiree could give her a little coaching."

"Okay, sounds like a plan," Terronez agreed. "Get her to sign a new contract and a copy of the new script. Let's see. Oh, yes. I can probably put off shooting the scenes with Gunner in them—that was the part which Mr. DeSalvo had before his unfortunate exit—but not for long. Any more suggestions? And, no, I will not play the role, so no comments on that idea from the peanut gallery."

The room was quiet for a moment before Rebecca Morton spoke up.

"I know a local comedian," she said. "His stage name is Uncle Brew. His comedy set is pretty good if you haven't seen it ten times. He's also done several local commercials."

"Uncle Brew," Geoffrey mused. "Terrible stage name, but if my little honey bunny likes him, we'll give him a try. Unless you've been sleeping with him."

There was a twinkle in his eye when he made the comment, but you could tell he was dead serious.

Rebecca blushed. "No, Geoffrey, and I'm not one to sleep around." She paused. "Well, at least not with just anyone." She smiled and kissed him on the cheek.

"I assume you know how to get a hold of him?" he asked.

"Yes," the marketing director said. "I've booked him for a few shows at the college."

"Excellent," the director said. "We'll resume filming tomorrow. I want everyone on the set by seven a.m. even if you're not in one of the morning scenes. Things are about to get serious, folks."

***

Desiree felt more nervous than usual as she finished getting ready for her date with Mick. Maybe she was making a mistake of getting involved so soon after the disaster she had experienced with Donald. Not to mention the early problems with the picture and all of the extra stress that was added.

But she did enjoy Mick's company.

She smoothed out the front of her pink breast-cancer-awareness t-shirt with a pink ribbon proclaiming, "Treasure Your Chest" and ran the brush through her hair one last time.

She heard Mick's car pulling up into the circular drive of House on the Hill just as she turned out the bathroom lights and grabbed her purse from the small table by the door.

There was a knock at the door and when she opened it, Mick was standing there with a single red rose in his hand. He wore a nice pair of white slacks and a neon blue shirt that made his eyes stand out even more. She smiled and accepted the rose.

"And just where did you find a rose this time of year in Northern Florida? I didn't see a flower shop in Angel Falls."

"I'll never tell," he said. "Maybe I'm a magician."

"Fine," she replied. "Guess we'll see just how magical a place called Swampy's Tavern can be, huh?"

***

It had cooled off enough so that there was a slight breeze on the patio of Swampy's. The breeze had that unmistaken smell of the ocean, and the sky was so clear that the stars and moon seemed to hang in the night sky as if suspended by invisible heavenly strands.

The meal had been very good although they had both avoided Swampy's Famous Fried Gator strips. Desiree had finished off her baked potato and corn-on-the-cob and biggie salad with ease.

Since then, they had been sipping their wine and trading life stories.

"I woke up at three o'clock in the morning to find three cats in my trailer sitting on my bed. I was sharing a trailer with Mayva who was our makeup lady for *Vampire Vixens from Outer Space*. The cats belonged to Mayva, but no one knew she had even brought them along. Heck, we were out in the middle of the desert miles

68

from anything. But suddenly, there I was in bed with three cats staring at me as if I was some creature from another planet. Mayva must have gone outside to have a cigarette. I swear that lady smoked five packs a day. But I guess the cats missed her and decided to keep me company. I must admit it was a bit creepy having them stare at me. I was afraid to close my eyes. I guess I thought if I did, they would pounce on me and tear me apart."

Mick laughed. "Not much of a cat person, huh?"

"Oh, no. I love cats. In fact, I'm a real animal lover. Way too many horror movie scripts though. When I see the mailman, I picture an axe in his mailbag. Heck, I saw a little old lady last week who I swore was following me with a pair of sharp knitting needles in her purse."

She stopped as he took another sip of wine and glanced up at the blue-black of the evening sky.

"Am I rambling?" she asked. "I hope I'm not boring you. I guess I'm just nervous. Besides, you probably read about the cats in one of my *Fangoria* interviews."

"Well, I did, but I enjoyed it hearing it in person much more."

"I'm sorry," Desiree said as she softly bit her lip. "Guess I'm just a little nervous."

"Who isn't?" he asked. "Dating is always such an awkward thing. My heart has been pounding in my chest so loud I thought for sure you'd comment on it. Either that or it was going to pop out of my chest and land on the table in front of you."

She laughed. "Not like it hasn't happened to me before, Mick. Of course, all the other ones have been props."

He smiled and refilled her wine glass.

"Thank you," she said. "Guess I've been talking your ear off all night. I think it's your turn now. You seem like much more than a "fix-your-air-conditioner" kind of guy. Not that there's anything wrong with that, of course."

He shrugged. "It's a job. I enjoy it and the pay's decent, but I lost most everything in the divorce except for the Viper. And I hope you don't think it's weird or anything, but I am a cat person."

"You don't mean a cat burglar, do you?"

He laughed.

"Well, that occupation might pay a little better and if I got caught, the accommodations might even be a shade better than the trailer I'm currently renting, but no, not a burglar."

"Cats, huh. That's cool if you don't have three hundred of them living in your trailer."

He shook his head. "Only one. I guess he's the one other thing I got in the divorce. His name is Lucky Lou. He's a longhaired chocolate-colored Maine Coon. I swear, his coat is softer and silkier than an expensive pair of panties from Victoria Secret."

"And just how would you know how expensive lingerie feels, Mr. Collins? You're not one of those perverts who wanders around the store claiming that they're looking for dainties for their wives, are you?"

"Hey," he answered with a wink. "Promise me that secret dies with you."

"So. Lucky Lou?"

"Yep. I bought him and my wife divorced me a week later. Best thing that ever happened to me. Well, so far," he said with a sly look on his face. "He follows me everywhere I go, which isn't typical for a cat. Either he likes me a lot or I smell like Starkist Tuna all the time. I can barely sit down to write before he's sitting on top of my desk."

"Write?"

Even in the shadows of the dim patio lighting, she thought he blushed.

"Sorry. I know. Everyone you talk to is either handing you a movie script or writing the next great American novel."

"So, which is it? A novel or a script?"

"Maybe it's a how-to-repair-your-plumbing nonfiction book," he teased.

"Is it?"

"No, it's a novel," he admitted. "I don't really like to talk about it. I've been working on it for years. My wife said I was stupid to waste my time on it, so that sort of put a dent in my ego, but I've been working on it quite a bit the past few weeks."

"Mick, I think that is so cool. I could never write fiction. I'm having a hard enough time writing my memoirs."

"*Memoirs of a Scream Queen.*"

"That's the one. It's not even finished, and my publisher has already started publicizing it. Sort of puts the pressure on and takes the fun out of it to some extent. But what can you do? You sign the contract, cash the check for the advance and then stress about it until it's finished. But tell me more about your novel, Mick."

"The working title is *Die Laughing*. It's sort of a revenge action horror story. I've always sort of pictured John Malkovich as the main character."

"Catchy title. What's it about if you don't mind me asking?"

He shrugged. "It's about a guy named Lester Sharp. He doesn't come across as the brightest bulb in the room which is why I went with that name. Les Sharp. Get it?"

"I like it. Very clever. You start picturing the guy immediately just with his name."

"Anyway, Les is always getting bullied in high school by three goons. It goes on for every year of school. Week after week. Month after month. Doesn't do much for the guy's ego, you know? So, after high school everybody moves to different parts of the country. Les is scarred by the years of bullying and can't get a good job. Eventually he gets a job as a clown with the circus. And, of course, he finds that he can't even hide behind his clown make-up as even little kids seem to run away from him in tears as they hide behind their mother's skirts. For years, he goes on the road, going from town to town searching for the three bullies. He ends up killing them off one by one and dresses them all in clown costumes. That's why I call it *Die Laughing*. I enjoy the writing, but I'm not sure if it is good enough to ever get published."

"If you'd like me to, I'd be glad to read what you have done. No promises, but if I like it, I'd have no problem mentioning it to my publisher, Coven Press."

"I don't know," he said. "I really wouldn't want you to feel obligated."

"I already said 'no promises.' Really, it wouldn't be any trouble. What was Blanche DuBois say in *A Streetcar named Desire*? Something like 'I have always depended on the kindness of strangers.' That's been my entire movie career in a nutshell. This will be a nice break from all those bad scripts I have to read all the time."

"Well, if you really don't mind. I have no clue how all this works. I just sit down and write. It would be nice to get a second opinion. So, shall we get out of here before the mosquitoes begin dive-bombing us?"

She nodded and waited while he paid the bill. He took her hand as they walked back to his Viper and her heart beat a little faster. He was right. Dating never did get any easier no matter how old you were.

"I'd like the top down if you don't mind," he said as he helped her in.

"Mr. Collins. Shame on you," she teased. "It's going to take more than a couple of glasses of wine for that to happen."

Mick laughed and gave her a quick peck on the cheek.

She took a quick breath and squeezed his hand before he closed her door and got in on the driver's side.

He put his keys in the ignition and lowered the top. "Do you hate the dating game as much as I do?" he asked.

"Well, it can certainly be a little awkward at times, but there's nothing more romantic than those first few dates with a new person. I know you were married for several years, but you surely remember the magic of your first dates even if you hate her guts now."

He laughed. "I guess that's true."

"So where does a guy take his dates around here other than Swampy's Tavern?"

"Well, not much around here anymore. Seaside Slide amusement park was always high on the list though."

"So, let's go there," she suggested

"Sorry. It's not open any more. Been closed for several years."

"Has it been torn down?"

"Amazingly, it hasn't," he replied.

"Then, let's go. Sounds like an adventure."

"Well, it's all locked up, but I guess I could put my cat burglar skills to the test."

***

The amusement park sat on a bluff overlooking the Atlantic Ocean. It was dark and desolate and seemed like it would be the perfect set for a horror movie.

Unable to pick the lock on the front gate, Mick had boosted

Desiree over the top of the gate and then climbed over himself. She felt a tingle go through her body when his hand rested briefly on her rear end as he helped her over.

He pointed out a few of the park's highlights.

"That eight-story water slide over there was the area's biggest attraction," he said as he pointed to an imposing slide which now looked as if it might topple over with the slightest breeze from the ocean. "It was the biggest waterslide in Florida. But for some reason, people started heading up to St. Augustine or down to Daytona Beach. Of course, the spring breakers used to love Daytona. Guess the Angel Falls student didn't want to stay in their own backyard when it came to spring break. Now I hear Lauderdale is the cool place to go."

They walked along the fence, hand in hand.

"That's the Speed Demon over there. The girls hated it. The guys loved it cause the girls always ended up in the guy's arms before it was over. Spook Central is right over the rise there. It was a typical haunted house."

"Bet it's even scarier now," Desiree said.

He nodded. "Probably, although you'd likely end up falling through the rotted flooring. The Florida humidity is not too kind to abandon dwellings. And over there is the Silly Silo, the Scrambler, Pharaoh's Fury and finally, the infamous Hell on Wheels, one of the few wooden roller coasters around at the time. Most of the new coasters have gone to steel tracks as it allows them to do crazy twists and turn upside down. But there's nothing like a wooden coaster track."

He sighed and Desiree could feel nostalgia through his voice and touch.

"And here's the old lighthouse. It really wasn't used for ships or anything. More of an attraction. People could walk to the top and have a great view of the cove and the beach."

He kept walking until Desiree stopped and tugged at his arm.

"Let me see your right hand," she said.

"What?"

"Your right hand. My grandma was a fortune teller, you know."

"You're going to check my lifeline and see how long I'll live or tell me who my next true love will be or maybe if I'll get a novel

73

published?"

"Well, I'm not that good," she said as he held out his hand. She studied it in the dim light of the moon for a moment. "Hmm. Looks like you are practical and prudent; ambitious and disciplined; patient and careful; humorous and reserved, and--"

"And what?"

"Possibly a little turned on?" she said as she placed a kiss onto the center of his palm.

He cleared his throat. "Possibly..."

She closed his hand and smiled up at him. "So, is that cove a romantic place?"

"Very," he said. "Would you like to see it?"

"Sure," she said. "But only if you kiss me first."

"Wow, you're not a very good blackmailer, are you?" he asked and then he took her in her arms and kissed her. Lightly at first, then again. The kisses started out tenderly but became more passionate with each one.

She laughed and broke away. "Race you to the beach!"

And before he knew what was happening, she was off and running.

By the time he caught up with her she had already kicked off her sandals and shed her T-shirt as well.

By the time their toes touched the water, they were completely naked, their clothes scattered like Hansel and Gretel clues all the way down the beach.

The crash and roar of the evening tides told the rest of the story.

***

"Come on, baby," Michelangelo pleaded with Rio Ruiz.

He was waving an empty beer can in one hand and using the other arm to keep from falling on his face. "Just stay the night. We'll have a good time, I promise."

"I came over here just to make sure you were okay after everything that has happened," she snapped. "I didn't come over here for a night of hanky-panky or whatever it is you Americans call it. I must get up early and then spend four hours to get my zombie make up on. It's only a small part in this film, but I'm not going to let that."

"Hey, if it's a big part you are looking for, make you came to the right place," he muttered grabbing his crotch.

"You're despicable, you know that? Your girlfriend is missing and all you care about is trying to sleep with me! You are a low life sleaze!"

"Well, to hell with you too, little lady," he said as he jerked his hand for effect, sloshing his beer across the carpet. "I can find a better way to spend the evening anyway."

"I'm sure you can," she said as she stepped out of his room and into the courtyard. "I'm sure you and your hand are very good friends."

And then she was gone.

Michelangelo grabbed another warm beer from the six-pack and staggered towards the bed. "It's just you and me, Bud," he said and promptly spilled half of the can as he opened it.

***

"Huh, what?" Michelangelo woke up a couple of hours later, still very drunk, and disoriented. The TV was still on and some infomercial about vacuum cleaners was explaining how good their suction was. It made him giggle. He reached for another can of beer, but then realized they were gone. Which also explained why he desperately needed to take a piss. He staggered to the bathroom and after a couple of shakes, he zipped up and didn't even bother to flush the toilet.

He caught movement from the corner of his eye and smiled.

"Rio? Is that you? Changed your mind about a little Italian lovin', eh?"

There was another flicker of movement. He spun around in a full circle but saw nothing and nearly lost his balance.

"Come on, Rio. If you want to play games, I have a much better one in mind. It involves placing Part A into Part B if you get my drift."

He laughed again and jerked aside the shower curtain. Still nothing.

But then he heard something. He looked up and the sight simply didn't register, especially behind the haze of the six-pack. There seemed to be a naked lady suspended from the bathroom ceiling from something that looked like a spider's web.

"Whoa. Cool trick," he said. "Are you with Circus Ole or something? To hell with Rio. We can have our own little party. I'll even bet you're double-jointed, aren't you?"

When the lady smiled, her lips pulled back to reveal fangs and her eyes slowly turned from dark brown to a bright red.

"Very cool," Michelangelo muttered and hardly felt the pain as she dropped from the ceiling and sank her fangs deep into his throat.

"The evil murmurs of the night
Grow louder before dawn's light
In the darkness they whisper
"You're not one of us" –
Am I going crazy?
There's no one I can trust"
-*Michael McCarty*

X

Zyana

(Part Two)

The Journey

Zyana knelt her aching knees before the heat of the bonfire that had been built in the center of their camp. She held a candle in her hand, the hot wax dripping down over her arm. She whispered a prayer and gazed towards the evening sky.

She was worried.

It had been weeks since they had escaped from Tenochtitlan, traveling through strange lands, and meeting native tribes both friendly and fierce. They had lost three acolytes and two slaves in battles and now many more lay deep with sickness around the fire. Healthy slaves continued to add wood and dry brush to the fire in the hope that the extreme heat would drive the evil spirits which had invaded their bodies.

Zyana sat down in the candle and picked up a clay pot filled with herbs the acolytes had foraged from the surrounding jungles. She lifted Noctalyc's head and forced some of the liquid down his throat.

He coughed, then opened his watery eyes.

His voice was weak from two weeks of being under the spell of sickness. "And now you try to poison me?" he whispered.

Zyana smiled. "You live, notahtzin."

His own smile was weak. "I think your diagnosis is premature." But his spirit was lifted when she used the Aztec term for father. She had never done that before.

He tried to sit up, but she put a hand on his chest and gently pushed him back down.

"Where are we?" he asked.

"The native guide says we are near the sea. Do we continue our journey in the direction of the rising sun?"

"We must," he said as his voice grew weak from talking. "How many survive?"

She managed to have a small smile. "Well, if you live, old man, perhaps a dozen acolytes and three or four slaves. But we can always pay for more slaves. Our treasure coffers are still plentiful."

"At lease those who have passed are in the land of the blessed," he said as his eyes closed again.

"The gods have forsaken us," she cursed. "The souls of our people are rotting in the dirt as we speak."

"Do not be blasphemes, my child. The Spaniards are already our enemy. No need to make enemies of the gods as well."

And then he was asleep again.

She was still awake and at his side when he woke in the morning.

"Do you never sleep?" he asked as she lifted a cup of water to his lips.

"Queens do not have time to sleep," she replied. "But while you were being lazy and having visions of virgins in your dreams, I was discovering more information about your magic fountain. The locals have heard the stories too."

His eyes brightened. "They have heard of the Fountain of Life?"

"They have heard the tale from conquistadors passing through. The Spaniard bastards call it the Fountain of Youth."

"That is wonderful news," he said, his spirits lifted by her words.

"It lies in a land the Spanish have named La Florida. It is a peninsula at the eastern edge of our world and still many months of travel from our current location."

She hesitated.

"What is it you are not telling me?" he asked.

"The legends they have heard say it may not be a fountain of life, but a portal to the underworld and that Xolotl resides there to guide souls through the levels of Hell."

The priest shivered. "I do not believe this," he said fiercely. "I have heard rumors of the fountain of life since I was a child. We must believe it exists. It is the only chance for the Aztec empire to rise again."

"We shall see," she replied. "If this fountain brings eternal youth, I can simply wait and bring destruction down on the Spaniards at any point I choose in the future. If it is a portal to the underworld, then I may follow it as my life will no longer have meaning. I live only to destroy the Spaniards."

"These guides have agreed to lead us to this land called La Florida?" the priest asked after a fit of coughing.

"We are negotiating with them at this very moment," Zyana said, and the screams of the negotiations could be heard in the background. "I am sure they will agree to do what is in their best interests."

She wiped the sweat from the heat of the fire from her forehead and stood up.

"Then we will find this magic pool if it takes us years. And once I bathe in this pool I can wait for a year, a decade or even a century to rain destruction down on the Spaniards and their descendants.

"I hope you get what you wish for, my Queen. But you must keep your heart clean. You must not let the temptations of darkness enter your soul."

"Is revenge dark, my father?" she asked. "Or rather, is it simply colored in bright red . . . ?"

The Aztec Queen smiled and curled up in her blanket and waited for dreams of power and glory to fill her heart.

Part Three

Evil Screams

"Creatures move within the night
With fangs and claws and fatal bites.
They cut and slash with sheer delight,
Then fade away,
In shades of gray,
Devoid of any light."
-Stan Swanson

XI

Night Moves

It was very late when Desiree and Mick pulled up into the circular drive of the 150-year-old House on the Hill mansion. As the lights of the Viper illuminated the exterior of the building, the place looked like one of those creepy dwellings you'd see in '60s horror sitcoms like *The Addams Family* or *The Munsters*. Or perhaps one of those movie sets where you knew at least a half-dozen scantily dressed sorority girls were going to meet their bloody end at the hands of a slasher.

"When can I see you again?" Mick asked as he reached over and pushed a strand of hair out of Desiree 's eyes.

She touched his hand before he could withdraw it and smiled. "Not as soon as I'd like," she admitted. "Looks like I'll be shooting for two more days before I get my next break. How does this weekend sound?"

"Well, I guess that will have to do. I made a great baked vegetable lasagna. And Lucky Lou can decide whether he likes you or not?"

"And if he doesn't?"

"Well, then he's not as smart as I gave him credit for. Plus, he hasn't been neutered, so I can always threaten him with that."

She laughed. "Well, he should be neutered anyway. Must be a

guy thing."

They kissed one last time, lingering for just a moment, then Desiree quickly exited, resisting the urge to look back. Without bothering to turn on the dorm room lights, she headed straight for the shower and relaxed under the warm sting of the spray.

I could sleep for a week, she thought.

Unfortunately, she knew she had to be on the set early the following morning.

She quickly toweled off and then crept into the sleeping area of the dorm so she wouldn't wake Gina. It didn't take her long to discover that her friend was still awake. And so was the other person in bed with her.

"Oh, Jeez, Gina, I'm sorry. I didn't realize—"

Gina laughed. "No problem. Guess I could have put a pair of my panties over the doorknob or something."

Another head popped out from beneath the sheets. "I'm sorry, too," the girl said. "It was so late that we thought you might not be coming back here tonight anyway."

Desiree squinted in the dim light. "Is that you, Barbara?" The two had met on the set previously that day and the Scream Queen knew that Gina was helping the newbie with her lines. Apparently, that offer of help extended quite beyond the reading of lines.

"Yep, the one and only Barbara Quincy" the girl replied. "I can head back to my own room if you'd like."

"Don't worry about it," Desiree replied to the shapely blonde. "But I am curious. I've been trying to place you since the first time we met. It seems like I should know you from somewhere."

The blonde shrugged. "Not sure. I was with an all-girl band a long time ago, but that's about it."

"That's it!" Desiree exclaimed. "You were the lead singer of that Goth band. What was it now? Oh, yeah, Barbara and the Bee Girls."

Barbara laughed, but you could tell she was delighted. "I can't believe you remember our band. That seems like another lifetime ago. I was still in my teens when we hit our peak. Of course, it didn't last long, but I sure enjoyed it."

"I still sing 'My Cannibal Boyfriend,' in the shower," Desiree admitted. "That was such a great tune. Why didn't you stick with it?"

"Just another 'one trick pony' band, I guess. It seems like we played every mall in America for two years to promote that song. But all the record company wanted to know was 'where is your next hit?'. We were writing some good stuff, but they just didn't feel it was commercial enough. The group split. I did a solo CD, but it never sold enough for me to stay in the business. I was running out of cash and Playboy had been bugging me to do a spread for months just because I had a recognizable name and a decent set of knockers. I said, 'why the hell not' and did a shoot. Turns out it was the best thing I ever did as it got me noticed by Geoffrey Terronez and here I am."

Gina groaned. "Now that I've heard your life story for the second time tonight, my love, can we get some sleep?"

The trio of scream queens laughed, and the room finally grew quiet.

Desiree fell asleep wishing she hadn't washed off the scent of Mick's cologne, but at least she had some very nice dreams for a change.

***

Geoffrey Terronez slipped on one of his new bathrobes (this one had been imported from New Zealand) as he walked across his suite to answer the door.

It's after midnight, he said to himself, this had better be good.

He opened the door prepared to fire whoever was standing there on the spot. He hesitated when he saw it was Rio Ruiz. Not only was she stunningly beautiful, but there was a worried look on her face.

Now what, he wondered.

"Did I wake you, Mr. Terronez?" the Brazilian actress asked.

"Does it make a difference, my dear? I am standing here wide awake, so it apparently does not. Now, did I need to pour myself another Scotch or do you have something more interesting to offer?"

Rio didn't understand the implications of what he was suggesting, so he just rolled his eyes and invited her in.

"What is it, Miss Ruiz?" he asked wearily. "It's not that I don't mind a beautiful girl at my door, but it's late. And even I, the great

Geoffrey Terronez, need my beauty sleep."

"I am worried about Michelangelo DeSalvo, sir."

"That idiot? And just why should he concern me? In case you haven't heard, I fired him today."

"I know. But I was sort of worried about him. I heard he had been drinking a lot, so I went to see him. We had an argument, of course. It is hard to be logical with someone who is drunk. Of course, I was still worried. Guess I got that from my own mama. I dropped back later, and his door was wide open, and no one was there."

"Well, he probably just decided to pack his stuff and head back to Italy. His movie future here is certainly dead. Lucky for him there are still lots of Italian horror film makers."

"No, Senor, I mean, Mr. Terronez. His things are still there, and I saw what I thought was some blood on the floor in the bathroom. I am truly worried."

"Fine, fine," Terronez said as he ushered her toward the door. "I'll notify security. Now, we all have an early morning, so I suggest you get back to your room and catch a few winks."

"Winks, sir? What exactly is winks?"

"Sleep," he said forgetting her English still needed work. "Get some sleep. I'll take care of all of this. Thank you."

And before she could say another word, she was standing outside and the door to his suite closed.

Hell, if I'm going to call security, the director told himself. With my luck they'll shut down production. Especially with everything that has happened in the past.

"Three people missing in three days," he whispered in the darkness of his suite. "Shit!"

And this time he hadn't had anything to do with it . . .

***

Most paparazzi have surveillance equipment that would put any local police department to shame. That wasn't the case, however, with Greg Dane, who currently sat in his room at the Motel 99 pondering his next move.

His equipment consisted of an old pair of binoculars that had been used by his grandfather in World War II and a glass cup. But it was all he had needed.

He was all smiles.

A glass cup against the thin wall between his unit and that of Geoffrey Terronez had been all he had needed. The small bribe to rent the room next to the director had paid big in dividends.

When he heard the door in the room next to his close, Dane went into his bathroom and pulled out his cell phone.

"Aimee, this is Greg Dane." He paused. "Yes, Snoopy. Whatever. Just listen. How soon do you think you can book a flight that will get you somewhere close to Angel Falls, Florida? Why? I have the scoop of the year here if you remember the arrangement, we made a few days ago. Let me know when and where your flight arrives, and I'll pick you up. I'll give you the details on the ride from the airport. What? No, you won't be wasting your time. I think I just might have made both of our careers a little brighter no matter how this whole thing plays out. Either Geoffrey Terronez is going to jail or there is something even bigger going on here. The sooner you get here, the better, my dear."

***

Roland sat at his desk and tried to look as much like a university president as he could.

"Come on," Rebecca Morton moaned. She checked the previous shot on the expensive Canon digital camera (technically belonging to the college although it was usually in her office or her house) and shook her head. "I've seen better mug shots of drunk Hollywood actors and country singers!"

"I'm tired," he replied. "Can't this wait?"

"The AFU Alumni Magazine is nearly ready for the printer. Now if you want your friggin' photo on the cover, then smile. Otherwise, I might as well go shoot one of the half-naked zombies over on the set. Now that I think about it, we might get more contributions that way. Now give me a smile that shows me you aren't attending a funeral."

"Why him?" he asked, ignoring everything she had just said.

"I assume you are referring to Geoffrey Terronez?"

"Well, you are sleeping with him."

"Well, Roland," she replied. "Who I share my bed with is really none of your concern. Things don't last forever. Besides, I'd think you'd be more concerned with what your wife might think if she ever found out we were, well, messing around. Now, can we get this done please?"

Roland's smile was about as warm as an hour old burrito, but it was still the best photo she had gotten all morning. They were both relieved when the intercom on his desk buzzed.

"Sorry to interrupt you," his secretary said, "but Mr. Doonan says it's important."

"No problem, Laura," he replied. "We were just finishing up. Go ahead and send him in."

Rebecca and Paul Doonan exchanged pleasantries at the door and the university's vice president hobbled in. Roland rolled his eyes as the man slowly made his way across the room, a cast on his foot and crutches under his arms.

"Well, well," Roland smirked. "If it isn't Hopalong Cassidy. And don't give me any grief about that being before your time. You're older than I am."

Doonan simply handed him several sheets of paper stapled together.

"What's all of this this?"

"It's the bills from the hospital, the lab and three different doctors." he said. "I called our insurance plan, and it seems they won't even cover half of this. Not with the medical plan you put into place last year."

"So?" Roland asked, dropping the papers onto his desk.

"Well, it wasn't me that dropped a friggin' sarcophagus lid on my feet, was it?"

"I don't have time for this, Doonan," Roland snapped, his face growing red.

"Well, then make time. Take care of the bills and a month-long vacation to recuperate—the Bahamas would be nice—and no one will hear another word about this mysterious item you have hidden away in the science building."

"Jeez, you have more cojones than I gave you credit for," Roland said. "And what's a little blackmail between friends?" He got down on his knees and opened the safe behind his desk. He counted out several thousand dollars and tossed it on top of the desk.

"That ought to cover it," Roland said.

"Well, double that amount and I'll let you in on another piece of information you might want to hear about."

Roland studied the man's eyes for several moments, decided it wasn't time to gamble and counted out another stack of cash.

"This had better be good," he said, not exactly happy about depleting his "emergency" funds.

Doonan stuffed the cash into the inside jacket of his suit and smiled.

"Oh, it's good, alright. Sheriff Stroud is coming to the college tomorrow for a visit."

"Now why would she do that? I swear that bitch has been trying to screw me ever since, well, ever since we stopped screwing. So, what's the rest of the story?"

"Well, apparently Slim Jim, that's Atkins, head of security in case you forgot, contacted her about that actress, PJ what's-her-name that went missing, and mentioned your brother as well."

"That idiot. I thought we were paying security enough to handle crap like that and not go off calling the cops. When this is all over, remind me to fire him. Does she have a warrant?"

"Nope. Just a friendly visit, but if she gets too nosy, well, it will seem strange not to allow her access to the science building."

"Great. That is just friggin' great," Roland said. He thought about it briefly. "We need to get rid of that sarcophagus. My brother's truck, too. And we need to get those illegals off the campus for a few days."

"Isn't getting rid of your brother's truck tampering with evidence?" Doonan asked. "I think maybe we should—"

Roland slammed his fist down on the desk so hard the phone bounced into the air and the receiver came off the hook.

"I believe I just paid you enough money, so you don't have to think, Doonan. Now, if you still want to lay on the beach in the Caribbean for a month, you'll do exactly as I say. Got it?"

Doonan nodded quietly.

Roland grabbed a few more bills from the safe and stuffed them in his pocket. "Guess it's a good thing that the bank of Bannister has planned for a rainy day. I think the water level is already up to my ass. Now, before you send the workers away for a couple of days, let's get them to help move the sarcophagus onto

Randy's truck. I have a storage shed rented on the other side of Angel Falls. We can just park it there for now. Let's wait until dark. Have them meet me at the science building at eight o'clock tonight."

***

Roland and three Hispanic workers quickly loaded the empty stone coffin onto the back of Randy Bannister's pick-up truck.

The university president handed a roll of bills to Manny Lopez and the keys to the truck as well as the storage unit.

"Now, do you understand?" Roland asked as the other two workers waved and disappeared into the night. "Park the truck and don't come back to work until Monday. I'll get the keys back from you for the storage unit then."

"Got you, boss," Lopez said with a huge smile that irritated Roland more than he cared to admit.

No one should be that happy, the university president thought to himself.

Roland gave him a curt nod, then drove off towards his house in a golf cart.

Manny Lopez climbed into the cab of the truck. Stupid Americans, he thought, I would have done this for half the money. Dumb gringo doesn't even know I was born a half-mile from here. Wait until he gets my final bill.

He laughed and pulled a flask of tequila from his windbreaker.

There was a thud, like the branch of a tree had fallen on the roof of the truck, but there were no trees nearby. Maybe a piece of tile had fallen from the roof of the building.

He shrugged and started the ignition.

Who cares, he thought, it ain't my damn truck.

He shifted into first gear and glanced out the side window to make sure the dock door was closed and locked. Something suddenly had him by his hair and jerked him through the open window, dragging him to the roof of the truck's cab. The last thought in his head was that he should kept his hair much shorter.

Not that it would have done him much good.

A few moments later his body, drained of most of its blood, dropped to the hood of the truck, then rolled off into the gravel in front of it. The truck, however, was still in gear and as it moved

90

forward, rolled over the body with a loud crunch.

"Blondes have more fun
Brunettes have more guns
Redheads have more curves
Silver foxes have more nerves"
-Michael McCarty

XII

Blondes Have More Fun

Rio Ruiz sat in the courtyard of the university campus after making her way back from visiting Geoffrey Terronez in his Motel 99 suite. The evening was beautiful as a soft breeze from the ocean drifted through the campus and the palm fronds seemed to float magically in the dark sky of midnight. But all Rio could think about was that the director seemed unresponsive to the missing Italian actor.

Is this what it is like being an actor in America? she wondered. Maybe I should have stayed in Brazil. Rio is lovely this time of year...

She sighed, trying to decide whether to head back to her room or simply call a taxicab and head for the airport. Something was not right here. She had never believed all the stories she had heard about the famous American director, but now she was beginning to wonder. What other explanation could there be?

She heard the engine of a truck roar to life off to her right and wondered who might be up at this time of night. Then she laughed.

Here I sit wide awake in the middle of the night and wonder why someone is awake also, she thought. How silly. Probably crew members working on something for the set so that things will be ready to go in the morning.

But then she heard a crash and immediately stood up.

Without thinking, she ran towards the Science Building.

A red pick-up truck sat with its engine still running, but the front left fender was smashed in. It looked as if the truck had driven straight into the storage garage opposite the science building. She doubted if anyone had been hurt as the truck couldn't have been going very fast, but she still hurried over.

The clouds parted as she neared the truck and the moon revealed much more than she had expected to see. She stopped in her tracks.

A body lay beneath the truck and there was no doubt the man sprawled there, dressed in bloody work clothes, was dead. His skull had apparently been crushed by one of the vehicle's tires.

The mystery was how it had happened? There was no driver in the truck, and she saw no one else around. Had someone run over the helpless man and then simply run from the scene of the crime?

"Madre de Dios," she whispered as she crossed her heart. "I definitely should have stayed in Brazil..."

And it would have been a wise decision indeed.

The naked figure that walked slowly out of the darkness was mesmerizing. Like something out of a dream. Or a nightmare...

Rio couldn't move.

The woman's strong arms wrapped around her, and Rio could feel the firmness of the woman's bare breasts against her, but the flesh was not warm. At first the Brazilian actress thought the woman was going to kiss her on the neck, but then she felt sharp teeth slice easily through the skin of her throat.

And she knew she would probably never see the bright lights of Rio again.

***

Roland Bannister, dressed in a jogging suit that likely cost more than all the clothes hanging in an average man's closet, was sitting with a tall drink in his hand next to a beautiful new swimming pool.

He was surrounded by a dozen well-endowed topless zombie extras who were all listening to his every word as if hypnotized. He felt the fingers of one of the extras walking along his thigh, but knew he had to finish the story.

93

"Yes, ladies, I train every day," he said as the hand moved upward. "In fact, I just finished running the Boston Marathon."

"Isn't the Boston Marathon held in the fall?" a tall blonde asked as she removed her bikini top and let the twins have some fresh air.

"Usually," Roland replied. "But they changed it this year just for me as I have such a busy schedule. I am the university president after all. But I still find time to stay in shape and I run every day. It is, however, a little disconcerting when you go jogging at the local park and see a sign that reads 'Beware of Alligators.' But it does make you jog a little faster..."

The gaggle of women, who were all now totally naked, giggled like schoolgirls and crowded closer around him.

"We love your new pool, Mr. Bannister," they cooed. And now there was more than one hand on his thigh and he—

He rolled over and nearly fell out of bed.

"What the...?"

Roland struggled to get out of the tangle of bed sheets, knocking over his glass of water as he reached for the phone. In less than a minute, he was fully awake and images of naked women far from his mind.

"I'll be right there," he whispered.

***

Slim Jim Atkins reminded Roland of a cross between Don Knotts and a Sumo wrestler. How someone could be so full of nervous energy that it felt like he might spontaneously combust at any moment and still weigh over three-hundred pounds, seemed medically impossible.

The head of the Angel Falls University security department and Paul Doonan stood side by side in the parking lot of the science building. They were each holding flashlights as they inspected what looked like Randy Ballinger's pick-up truck. Roland pulled his golf cart up behind the truck and stepped out, still dressed in his silk pajamas although he had thrown on a long trench coat as well.

Why the heck is that thing still here? he wondered. He also noticed that the stone sarcophagus was still in the bed of the truck.

And where the hell was Manny Lopez?

And then he noticed all the blood and the body beneath the

truck.

Slim Jim ambled over as quickly as his 300-pound frame would allow.

"Mr. Ballinger," the man said, out of breath after only a dozen steps. "We really need to call the police, sir. But Mr. Doonan told me to call you first. I think we should call Sheriff Stroud immediately, don't you?"

Roland sighed. "Mr. Atkins. Weren't you working for minimum wage as a security guard for Walmart before you started here?"

"Uh, yes, sir."

"Do you like your new job and your nice salary?"

"Uh, yes, sir."

"Then stop thinking. Your job is to catch students smoking pot or streaking across the quad."

"But, sir—"

Roland walked away from him in mid-sentence and joined Paul Doonan near the front of the pick-up.

"What the hell is going on here, Paul?" he asked in a hushed tone as the security chief mumbled to himself and walked around in circles several feet away.

"No clue," the man replied. "Slim called me just a few minutes ago. The truck's engine was still running, but Manny clearly didn't run over himself."

"No shit, Sherlock. And the sheriff will know that as well. This is getting out of hand."

Roland brushed his short hair back, his brain jumbled with thoughts.

As he walked a short distance away, lost in his thoughts, a noise on the rooftop brought him back to reality with a start.

Some stupid squirrel, he thought.

He was turning back towards the truck when his feet slipped in something, and he crashed to the cement surface of the parking lot. He winced, his tailbone aching, then swiveled around to see what he had slipped in. Even before he touched it, he knew it was blood. Paul and Slim Jim hurried over to help him up.

"You, okay?" Paul asked.

Roland ignored him and turned to the security officer. "Go

back to your security room or the vending machines or wherever you spend your time and forget about all of this," he told Slim Jim.

"But, boss, I—"

"Shut up!" he spat as his face grew red, only inches away from the head of security. Slim Jim tried to ignore the spittle as the man yelled at him. "You are also going to call Sheriff Stroud and cancel tomorrow's visit. Tell her that the movie is behind schedule and that the director is threatening the town with a lawsuit or something if things are held up any longer. And that wouldn't be good for the town's economy or her upcoming bid for mayor either."

"But—"

Roland grabbed the man firmly by the collar. "I hear that the Walmart in Palm Harbor is hiring, Mr. Atkins."

And that was all it took.

The man nodded, tried to straighten his shirt and waddled away.

Once the head of security had disappeared into the darkness, Roland turned to Paul Doonan.

"I don't know what is going on here, Paul, but this ship is going to sink fast if we don't get a handle on things. Already three people have disappeared, or is it four? I can't keep track. And our friend Manny is lying over there run over by a ghost truck or something. Which brings me to my next point, why do we have a pool of blood clear over here twenty yards from the truck?"

Paul looked down and his mouth fell open, he was speechless.

"We're getting no help from him, Paul. Believe me on that one."

"Well, I can probably clean up most of the blood although I think my trip to the Caribbean might need to be extended a couple of weeks, but that truck is covered from top to bottom. Maybe run it through a car wash?"

Roland's face lit up. "Friggin' brilliant."

"What?"

"Did you leave the keys in the truck?"

"Yes—"

"Come on," he said, grabbing Doonan by the arm.

They grabbed the smashed-up body and hefted it into the back of the truck beside the stone sarcophagus. Roland pushed Doonan into the driver's seat and directed him past the science building and then off the dirt road running near the back of the campus.

"Turn here," he said pointing into the marshy forest to the right.

"What?"

"Turn the friggin' truck here!"

Doonan steered into the trees and over logs and who knew what else, then jammed on the brakes as they approached the swampy bog of what students referred to as The Black Lagoon.

They got out and, with the truck still running, Roland jammed a tree branch against the seat and the pedal, then jerked it into gear. The truck jumped forward and left the ground for a split second at the edge of the bog before it hit the water and sailed forward a few feet. It slowly began to sink.

It seemed to take forever.

"Jeez, Roland, I don't think it's going to go all the way under," Doonan moaned.

"Don't worry," Roland replied with a smile. "I did the same thing two years ago when that sophomore over-dosed. That VW Bug is still under there somewhere."

A moment later the truck sunk completely beneath the dark water and only a few air pockets bubbled to the surface.

He stuffed his hands into his coat pockets and laughed. "And that, Mr. Doonan, is why you are just a department Vice President, and I am the President of Angel Falls University. Oh, and don't forget to go back and clean up all that blood before daylight."

"And then I can start packing for the Bahamas?" the man asked, still a little stunned from everything that had just happened.

"Think again, Mr. Doonan. Too much going on around here for you to be taking trips down south."

"But... but you promised..."

"Well, my friend, that was before you got yourself implicated in a crime."

And Roland Bannister laughed all the way back to his house.

***

Geoffrey Terronez's eyes were bloodshot, and his head was pounding from too much booze and not nearly enough sleep.

Even after Rio had left in the middle of the night, it took him forever to clean up Michelangelo's room. Not only had he scrubbed away the bloodstains, but then he emptied the room completely so that everyone would think the Italian actor had left town. At least there would be no more questions about him.

He wore his darkest shade of sunglasses so the cast and crew would remain ignorant of his condition. Not that he hadn't directed many times with little sleep and more than a few nightcaps. But the less gossip, the better. The filming had already gotten off to a bad start.

He kicked off his sandals once he reached the soft beach and the cool morning sand felt good under his feet. And the negative ions from the air off the ocean was already making him feel better. He took several deep breaths as he approached the set for the morning shoot.

"Good morning," one of the curvy topless extras said as she bounced past him.

"Morning? I guess it is. But I'll reserve my opinion on whether it is good or not," the director muttered.

He sat down in the director's chair and groaned. Rebecca Morton had already set up a beach lounge chair and was lathering every inch of her body that was bare with suntan lotion. And there was a lot uncovered as all she wore was a narrow bikini top and a pair of white Capri pants that looked as if they had been painted directly onto her skin.

Geoffrey started to compliment her on her looks when music blared over the nearest dune and distracted him. The morning heat made the man's arrival seem like something out of the Sahara Desert. He could have passed for a Jimmy Buffet clone with his Key West garb including a gaudy Hawaiian shirt, baggy Bermuda shorts and flip-flops that barely remained on his feet. The music blaring from the boom box on his shoulder was far from a Jimmy Buffet tune though. It was some rap song that Geoffrey wouldn't have recognized the difference from a hundred other rap songs.

Rebecca jumped out of her chair. "Brew!" she shouted and ran awkwardly through the soft sand to give the man a hug. She nearly jerked his arm off as she pulled him along the beach to where Geoffrey sat.

Terronez didn't bother to stand but did extend his hand. "The great Uncle Brew, I presume?"

"The one in the same. Didn't know I had that big of a following."

Terronez shrugged. "Wouldn't know. Never heard of you myself but Rebecca seems to be a big fan."

Uncle Brew shrugged off the comment and smiled widely. "Sorry I'm late. Had a gig in Miami last night and just got back."

"Mind turning off the racket?" Terronez asked with a flip of his hand toward the boom box.

"Sure. Sorry. Sort of amps me up before a performance."

"I assume you've read the script a couple of times?"

"Several times," the comedian answered. "Sounds like I play Rambo with a boner."

The director laughed and decided he liked Uncle Brew a little more than he thought he would. "Good. I have a scene to shoot here on the beach and then we'll try to get your first scene done before lunch."

"Cool. Do you like my duds?"

Terronez studied him. "I guess, but my sister already has a camo outfit ready for you."

"I just thought this would be a change of pace."

Terronez scowled. Now a two-bit comedian was already making wardrobe suggestions. "Now, why the hell would a gun nut wear such bright clothes?"

"I had the idea on the flight back," Uncle Brew explained. "Gunner is anything but a typical Sly Stallone kind of guy. He wears bright colors. The colors distract the zombies just long enough so he can put a bullet in the center of their rotting foreheads."

"Whatever," the director muttered. "Why don't you go run through your lines with one of the extras while I get this scene in the can."

"In the can," Uncle Brew laughed as he walked away. "I love it. Real movie talk. Of course, 'in the can' means something quite different to a comedian in front of an audience."

Terronez sighed and rolled his eyes at Rebecca.

She placed a hand on his arm. "He'll be fine. Just wait and see."

The director got up to better survey the scene and waded into the shallow surf to get a better perspective of things.

"Sewer Rat!" he yelled.

The musician/actor came near the edge of the water, but didn't step in. He wasn't sure all of the built-up flesh on his body was waterproof and he had just spent two hours in makeup just so he would look normal.

"I just to make sure we are on the same page. Okay?" he asked the actor. "You will be running down the cove to that part of the beach where all the fake driftwood is stacked up. You start to run in the opposite direction when you see more zombies in that direction. You turn and begin running toward the camera, but by then the zombies that were chasing you in the first place have caught up with you and knock you to the ground. At that point, of course, I need lots of authentic screaming, so we don't have to overdub in editing. They will be devouring you, so should be a piece of cake."

"Lovely," Sewer Rat said tossing his cigarette butt into the ocean. "I just hope no one bites through the prosthetics and really chomps into me."

"Well, if so, don't stop. Might help with the authenticity of the screams."

The actor couldn't tell if the director was serious or not.

Before he had a chance to question the statement, the director was screaming and grabbing for his foot. The next thing the crew knew, he was falling face forward into the shallow surf, blood turning the water near him crimson as it washed to the shore.

"Get him out!" Rebecca yelled. "He's gonna drown in a foot of water!"

Two members of the camera crew pulled him from the water where he collapsed to the sand, moaning in pain.

Rebecca ran to him. "Geoffrey! Can you hear me?"

She shook him, but by now he had faded into unconsciousness. She took a quick look at his leg.

"Shit," she muttered. "He must have stepped on a stingray which reacted in self-defense. The barb is still embedded in his leg. Call 911. Now!"

"Aren't you supposed to pee on it?" someone asked.

"That's jellyfish," Rebecca said, "And even that isn't a great idea. Why the hell don't you guys include a medic on your staff?"

"Tight budget," someone told her.

"I need something to wrap up the wound. Anyone have anything relatively clean?"

She received no response, so simply removed her Capri bottoms and wrapped them around his foot. Whether someone got a good peek at her nearly invisible pink thong didn't matter much to her.

***

Desiree wasn't sure what she was going to do with a few free days. *Memoirs of a Scream Queen* was certainly waiting for more input on her laptop, but the mood to write was not there.

With Geoffrey Terronez laid up for a couple of days after his encounter with Floridian marine life, production ground to a halt. Several of the crew had headed for Orlando to visit Disneyworld and the Harry Potter addition at Universal, but Desiree declined the invitation.

She had spent a couple of hours at the hospital, but Geoffrey Terronez wasn't much of a conversationalist even when in the best of moods. So now she found herself wearing one of her new bikinis and taking in a few rays on the nearest secluded beach she could find. She had found an old copy of Shirley Jackson's *We Have Always Lived in the Castle* and began reading it for the fifth time.

Peace and quiet, she thought as opened the book, but a shadow suddenly loomed over her.

So much for a secluded beach, she thought.

Desiree lifted her shades briefly to see who had invaded her space.

Blake Smith stood above her, wearing a pair of baggy shorts and a new Panama hat. Mr. Twinks, his teddy bear (and constant companion), wore the exact same outfit.

I'll bet he spends more money on the bear's clothes than he does his own, she thought. And where in the world would a person find a miniature Panama hat just the perfect size?

"Good morning, Ms. Starr," the producer said politely. "Sorry to interrupt your solitude. Mr. Twinks and I were just taking a morning stroll and contemplating our future."

"Your future?" Desiree asked.

"Well, you might think I'm a bit daft—" he paused.

That just might be the understatement of the year, Desiree thought while the producer collected his words.

"Mr. Twinks and I think that this movie might be cursed. I'm thinking of pulling out my money and heading back to England."

"Cursed?" Desiree asked. "You mean as in some kind of a voodoo curse?"

"Well," he replied. "I mean we aren't too far from Haiti and all that voodoo stuff you hear about. I mean if you believe in that kind of thing. But voodoo or not, I've had this ominous feeling all week. Mr. Twinks too. I mean, I'm not one to abandon a ship just because there's some water on the deck. I've had my fair share of things go wrong with making movies over the years. But this film just feels wrong. Do you know what I mean?"

Desiree thought about it. "Yes, I know what you mean. I mean, I love the area and the cast and crew, but I've had my share of bad vibes too."

"Well, just my two cents worth," he said. "Again, sorry for the interruption. Be careful, my dear. I've grown very fond of you over the years and only wish you the best. Now if you'll excuse me, Mr. Twinks and I have some more thinking to do."

He tipped his Panama hat and walked slowly away. She heard him mumbling and wasn't sure whether he was talking to himself or his teddy bear.

Desiree sighed.

So much for relaxing, she thought.

***

Aimee Breeze stood in the bathroom of the motel room and combed her hair as she stared at herself in the mirror.

Why do I do this, she asked herself. Is it worth it? I might as well be selling my body on Hollywood Boulevard.

And changing planes three times hadn't helped her mood. She'd had an hour layover in Denver and then three hours in Orlando before flying to Daytona Beach. Greg Dane had met her at the airport and then it was another hour's drive to Angel Falls and the Motel 99. She had hoped to get some sleep, but Greg Dane wasn't about to postpone the first part of their agreement and had

102

his clothes off before she'd had time to close the front door of the motel room. At least the height-challenged paparazzi hadn't taken long to complete their bargain.

The TV entertainment reporter had then slept most of the day but was still feeling the full effects of jetlag and the uncomfortable surroundings. She put on some eyeliner and some rouge to cover the circles beneath her eyes before exiting the bathroom.

"Jeez, Greg, put some clothes on."

He laughed and reached for a crumpled pair of boxer shorts on the floor next to the bed.

"What did you do? Only bring one pair?"

He frowned, not having a clue as to what she was insinuating.

"I told you this would be worth your time," he said as he pulled on a stained t-shirt. Three people missing and they've barely started shooting. I don't see how the authorities can ignore this. I think this film will be shut down for good once Terronez leaves the hospital."

Aimee made sure to stay away from the bed where Greg was sitting and sat down on the chair at the room's small desk. "And what if Terronez has nothing to do with the missing people?" she asked.

"What? Are you crazy? It's the only logical explanation."

"What's his motive, Greg? What would he gain from having two of his actors disappear? Okay, I know he fired one of them, but still. And what about the President's brother? Why would he kill him? And PJ Bottoms was just another SQIT who he easily replaced."

"SQIT?"

"Scream Queen in Training," she explained.

"Okay, but I know how mad he was at Michelangelo DeSalvo."

"Big deal. Directors and actors have arguments and disputes all of the time. He'd worked with DeSalvo in the past and will probably work with him again at some point. Well, if he's still alive, I mean. And nobody knows whether anyone is dead or not. They're just missing. I just don't see any benefit for Terronez."

"Maniacs don't need a reason," Greg argued. "They do it, well, because they're deranged."

"That might be a great plot in a B-movie, Greg. But I can't go on national TV and say Geoffrey Terronez is a madman without more solid proof than what you heard through a motel wall. I thought you had more on the guy than this."

"I don't see another explanation," Greg said, somewhat disappointed that the sexy tabloid reporter wasn't in agreement with him. It probably also meant no more nookie time. "So maybe Mr. Twinks is likely suspect, huh?" he said sarcastically.

Aimee Breeze smiled. "Hey, you're getting good at these B-movie plots, sugar. The truth is, I think it is Desiree Starr."

Greg Dane nearly fell off the edge of the bed. "What?"

"First of all, PJ Bottoms was a rival of hers—"

"Rival?" Greg interrupted. "Desiree is twice the actress that PJ is... or was."

"Quit interrupting," Aimee spat. "Second, everyone knows she was sleeping her way to the top. Hell, Michelangelo and this Randy guy were probably her lovers and were threatening her with blackmail. I mean, look at the scene she caused at the premiere of Bullet City. What a loser."

"You're way off base, Aimee. Desiree doesn't sleep with every guy she meets. Just the opposite in fact. She's pretty picky."

"Well, just because she wouldn't sleep with you, Greg, doesn't prove anything. And don't believe everything you read. Or even write for that matter. I'm telling you that she slept her way to the top and is now killing to stay there. She went from being a Scream Queen to a drama queen, and now, to a killer queen. That's my angle, sonny boy. In fact, I'm going to get my *Entertainment Now* film crew down here tomorrow and start filming."

"Hey, we agreed we were in this thing together!" Greg said with a pout.

"We've already had our 'together time.' You're on your own."

Dane crossed his arms and sat there like a scolded child. "Fine," he said. "How about another roll in the hay just for old time's sake?"

"Sorry, sugar," she told him. "I don't have sixty seconds to spare."

"Fine," he said. "But if by some far-fetched chance it is Desiree, then be careful or I might be writing your obit."

Aimee laughed. "Hey, shorty," she said. "Everyone in my

family has lived to a ripe old age. No worries here."

She stepped out into the refreshing evening air and closed the door behind her. She took a deep breath, but never had the chance to let it go in the form of a scream as something grabbed her and dragged her up the side of the building.

Her last conscious thought was "almost everyone in my family lived to a ripe old age."

"Strange Plays
You got me running through a maze
It's not too promising
To be seen
Seen with you"
-Linnea Quigley

XIII

Missing

Geoffrey Terronez felt like he was caught in a revolving door by the time he left the Angel's Fall's medical center. Much of the past 24 hours was a haze and all he remembered from the encounter with the stingray was the intense pain. But the fog of drugs made things much better.

With his foot wrapped in heavy bandages and leaning awkwardly on a pair of crutches, the medical staff sent him on his way. They told him to keep off his feet for at least two days, then return to see how the wound was doing and to make sure the antibiotics were doing their job as prescribed.

Although the pain medications helped, Terronez was already concerned about the film and wasted production time. His sister, however, insisted he follow doctor's orders and convinced him he could make up time by taking advantage of the long summer days. It might cause problems with the actor's union, but he thought it was worth the risk. Most of the crew and cast members respected him and knew what was on the line.

At least he had plenty of new scripts (which was nothing new) to go through while he was bedridden, although he wasn't entirely happy with his new orderly. It wasn't that Uncle Brew (whom he soon found out was Barnaby Brewster who originally hailed from Davenport, Iowa) wasn't good at being orderly. In fact, he was very good. But his first choice, Rebecca Morton, said she was needed at the college and choices two through twenty were out of the question as they were young, well-endowed zombie extras who Rebecca immediately vetoed.

And the director couldn't argue with the fact that Uncle Brew (in addition to being a dishwasher, a cabbie, pizza delivery man, a janitor and a bouncer) had once been an orderly as well.

Terronez popped another pain pill and washed it down with two fingers of whiskey. Uncle Brew sat in the room's easy chair thumbing through a recent issue of *Monster Agogo Magazine* admiring some artwork of a clown, a cowboy and a ghost drawn by artist Larry Nadolsky. It was a strange combination of characters, but it was certainly intriguing.

He tossed the magazine onto the room's desk when someone knocked on the door and he got up to answer it. Recognizing Blake Smith, one of the producers of *College of the Living Dead*, he let the man in. The man had a suitcase in one hand and his teddy bear in the other. Strangely enough, the stuffed bear's luggage was an identical but smaller piece of luggage.

"A stingray?" the producer asked. "Well, at least you have another story to tell the pretty ladies, don't you? But I am sorry to hear about the accident."

Terronez smiled. "Thanks. I heard a rumor you were withdrawing from the movie. I guess the suitcase in your hand tells me that the rumors are true."

Smith nodded. "Sorry, Geoffrey. When I get these feelings, I don't argue with them."

"And your psychic probably has something to do with it too, right?"

Smith shrugged. "This world is much darker than you might imagine, Geoffrey. There's something about this film, but I certainly wish you the best and hope I'm wrong."

"No worries, Blake. I know you've already invested some money and lots of time. You'll still get a producer's credit. I'll just give Lu another job title in addition to the other half dozen she already has."

"No hard feelings?" Smith asked as he sat down the suitcase for a moment and extended his hand.

"Nah," Terronez replied. "Shit happens as they say. Besides, I might need your money and talents on my next film."

"Good luck," Blake said as he picked up his suitcase and left the room, closing the door behind him.

"Looks like you're having a bad struck of luck," Uncle Brew said.

"Well," Terronez said as he filled his whiskey glass to the brim. "Bad luck and me have been friends for a long, long time. But I'm still here, ain't I?"

Uncle Brew shrugged and returned to his chair. He pulled another magazine from his suitcase and Terronez noticed it was a copy of a men's magazine called Brazilian Boobs.

The comedian immediately opened the magazine to the centerfold.

"Wow," he said. "This chick looks just like Rio Ruiz."

Terronez held out his hand and Uncle Brew got up and handed him the magazine.

"Let me see." Terronez laughed. "Your numbskull. It looks like Rio Ruiz because it is Rio Ruiz."

Uncle Brew smiled sheepishly. "Guess I was too busy looking at things other than her face, boss."

Terronez laughed again, tossed the magazine back at the comedian and then took a big swig of whiskey. Between the alcohol and the drugs, he wasn't feeling much pain. He fell asleep with strange dreams of missing cast and crew members who were all attired in zombie make-up. Or maybe it wasn't makeup. Maybe they were real zombies. He woke up screaming when Miguel Torrez, his head all caved in from being run over, grabbed his sleeve and started to take a bite out of his arm.

"Damn horror movies," he muttered and reached for the bottle of whiskey one more time.

***

Roland Bannister spent most of the day hiding out in his office. He had told his secretary to cancel any meetings and to hold all phone calls. He was beginning to think that making the deal with the movie production company had not been the best idea he had ever had. In fact, he was afraid the new swimming pool (now half-constructed) would come back to haunt him. Maybe he wasn't being as careful as he should have been.

He felt better after reviewing (and making several changes) to the school budget for the upcoming year, so it hid most of his personal expenditures. It took most of the day, but he felt better once it was done and decided to take the long route back to his house. The fresh air would help clear his mind.

Unfortunately, the route took him around the far side of the campus, and he regretted the decision the moment he approached the area of algae covered body of water where they had disposed of his brother's truck and the body of Manny Lopez.

Sounds from the boggy area seemed different to him as the evening approached and he even debated backtracking instead of continuing his trek.

"Don't be silly," he whispered, and his words seemed to drown in the depths of the bog.

There was a distinct rustling in a group of shrubs and bushes off to his left that took his breath away. He glanced around and grabbed a good-sized rock from the edge of the path to use as a weapon.

Roland was barely able to restrain himself from tossing the rock as Slim Jim Atkins stepped from the bushes and adjusted the zipper of his uniform.

"Hey, boss," the overweight security guard greeted. "Just making my rounds when nature called."

The university's president took a deep breath and cursed at the man. "Damn it, Jim. We have bathrooms all over the campus. The Ziegler Science Building is only a hundred yards away. And you must have just come from the Truesdal Library or the Founder's Hall area. What if school was in session and students were on this path?"

"Sorry, chief. Guess I wasn't thinking. I promise never to do it again."

Roland shook his head. "Just see to it that you don't."

"You know," Atkins said. "I never did hear what happened last night. I saw the truck and the body were gone. I hope you're not getting us all in trouble..." And then he added, "Sir."

"I don't recall a truck or a body, Atkins," Roland said. "And I don't believe that Mr. Doonan has any recollection of that either.

Do you? Now think carefully."

Slim Jim scratched his head until the light in his eyes suddenly clicked on. "Oh, yeah, that's right. I don't remember that either," he said softly.

"Just get back to work, Mr. Atkins."

The plump (Roland would have called him fat but knew that wasn't politically correct these days) security guard sauntered off toward the AFU Mission Bookstore.

The university president shook his head and then glanced over at the slimy green water and thought about his brother's truck that now lay at the murky bottom along with Manny Lopez's body. He was wondering if perhaps they should have weighed the body down, he knew the truck stay on the bottom because of the heavy stone sarcophagus in the back but was distracted when the bushes to his right rustled.

"Geez," he mumbled. "Can't anyone around here learn to use the bathrooms instead of the bushes? Who's there this time?"

The woman who stepped onto the path in front of him was completely naked except for a glittering array of jewelry that sparkled in the new moonlight.

"So, now everyone is using the bushes as a bathroom and a place to get laid? Who's back there with you? I swear if Michelangelo Desalvo is still here..."

But, as Roland soon found out, there was no one else in the vicinity.

He held up the rock for protection, but it was useless as a weapon against her.

***

Desiree sat at the table in Mick's kitchen in the cozy little cottage he rented near the beach.

"Nice place," Desiree said as they waited for the vegan lasagna to finish baking.

"Well, the rent is outrageous, but the view is worth it. Plus, I can jog down to the beach any time I want. I figured I owed myself a couple of little luxuries after the divorce. Sometimes I just feel old, you know. Sometimes I think I might have Dyslexia-Gem-Psychosis."

"Jeez, that sounds scary. What the heck is it?" Desiree asked

110

with concern.

"It's when the brain gets your age backward. I'm 44, but sometimes my brain thinks my body age is 64."

Desiree laughed. "Well, if that's true, sweetie, that means you will have the body of a 17-year-old when you are 71."

They both laughed. At that moment, Lucky Lou jumped from the kitchen floor onto Desiree 's lap. At first, she was startled until she realized it was only the cat. She was a real animal lover, and the cat immediately began purring in response to her stroking his soft fur.

"Wow," Mick said. "He's usually not that affectionate. It took him a couple weeks before he did that with me."

She winked. "Good thing it didn't take me two weeks to become affectionate towards you. Right?"

He blushed but was saved when the oven timer began buzzing.

***

Uncle Brew took a box of donuts from the sack of groceries he had brought back to the motel room after he had refilled Geoffrey Terronez's prescriptions. He opened the box and offered one to the producer who politely declined.

"Day old donuts are the best," he said between bites of the bear claw he had chosen to start with. "I don't know why know they sell them cheaper. They should be more expensive. You know, like fine wine. They taste better with age. Well, maybe not a week later, but you know what I mean."

"Your wine has to age at least a week before you drink it?" Terronez asked.

Uncle Brew laughed. "Hey, I'll have to work that into my next show. You know, and I hate to ask under the circumstances, but I'm thinking about trying my hand at writing a script."

"You and every other person I meet," Terronez muttered.

Uncle Brew ignored the comment. "It would be about a guy without hands called The Hands of Mime."

"So, if he doesn't have any hands, why would you use that title?"

"Well, it's a play on words. You know—the hands of time."

"And it's about a mime?" Terronez asked.

"I don't know," the comedian replied. "It's just an idea."

111

"Well," Terronez advised him. "Maybe you should think again."

Uncle Brew shrugged. "Want to watch some television? I think they're showing *Zombie Strippers* on one of the cable channels."

Terronez winced. "I can't believe that Robert Englund took that part when he could have been in *Blood Brothel Mama*. And Jenna Jameson should have stayed in the porn business. I think I'll pass."

"Okay, how about hearing some of the new jokes I'm thinking about putting into my next show?"

The director thought about it. "Well, I'm already in pain, so I suppose it can't get much worse."

Uncle Brew cleared his throat. "You know, old sayings are the weirdest things. I mean, they say that the early bird gets the worm. Well, if that's the case, why doesn't the worm just sleep in? Or, how about this one. Early to bed and early to rise, makes a man healthy, wealthy and wise—" the comedian paused for effect— "and pretty damned boring if you ask me."

Terronez gave him a puzzled look. "And you make a living doing this?"

"You betcha. I've got a gig in Albany next week. Let me think for a moment. Oh, yeah, how about this one. Nobody liked me when I was a kid. I swear. Even my imaginary friend wouldn't play with me."

The director smiled. "Okay, that's a little better."

This encouraged the comedian. "So, you tell me. Was the Wicked Witch of the East the first homewrecker?" He paused, then added. "Well, technically, I suppose the house wrecked her. Hey, where's my drumroll? Okay, try this one: is it true that the Wicked Witch from the South was a redneck?"

Terronez groaned and reached for his bottle of Scotch. Uncle Brew didn't slow down. "So, if you only drink half a 5-Hour-Energy drink, will it only give you two and half hours of energy?" The comedian cleared his throat one last time and said, "My doctor only gave me a week to live if I don't give up sex. Know why? Because I was screwing his wife."

Geoffrey grimaced, reached for the remote and turned on the television.

"What channel did you say *Zombie Strippers* was on?"

**

Mick's lasagna was delicious and went perfectly with the Merlot he brought out.

"For special occasions," he said.

"And what's the special occasion?"

"You're here in my place and my cat hasn't scratched your eyes out."

She laughed, but Mick could tell she was troubled.

He decided to change the subject, lighten the mood. "Doing those love scenes in movie make you hot?" he asked.

"Not really," she said nonplus.

"Really?"

"It is all an illusion."

"An illusion," he repeated.

"When I was in high school, I was a local magician's assistant. I wore a skimpy outfit and assisted him in his tricks on stage. The lighting, the smoke, it all created an illusion that the magic is real. It is same thing with bedroom scenes in film, illusions to create the magic."

"The nakedness, the moaning, the orgasms."

"Illusion, Illusion and illusion."

"Wow."

"We are not actually naked during the love scenes. Scantily dressed, but not completely without some clothes or covers hiding our more intimate parts, but it is also done with camera angles and cutting.

"The beds are usually just props, not real mattresses and the bedroom is full of people – the director, the camera crew, lighting people, sound crew and runners. Sometimes a producer will stop by.

"Every movement of the body is meticulously choreographed like a fine dance sequence. Many things to memorize and marks to hit and everyone in the room is watching you do it. In the end, you created magic, like that magician I worked back for in high school, but this time on the silver screen or TV."

"I'm not sure I will watch a sex scene the same again."

She laughed, but it was more a polite laugh this time.

"What's the matter?" he asked.

She was somewhat startled that he had noticed.

"Just looking at the driftwood out your front window. You know, driftwood is so pretty at first glance, but it always makes me kind of sad."

"Sad? Why would it make you sad?"

"Well, it used to be a living thing. A tree with bright green leaves. Maybe it floated in from the Bahamas or, heck, maybe as far away as Africa. And now it will never be able to go home again."

"Is that how you feel sometimes?" Mick asked.

She smiled but didn't answer.

"More Merlot?" he suggested as he lifted the bottle.

"I don't think so, Mick. I sort of feel like going back to my room and getting some rest. It's been quite the week. Give me a lift back to the university?"

"No problem," Mick said although he seemed a little disappointed.

As they drove away from the cottage he glanced back at the piece of driftwood in the sand. And suddenly, he did feel a little sad. He was a little sad that Desiree was going back to her room, but even more sad when he realized she would be flying back to California in just a couple of weeks.

Stupid piece of driftwood, he thought as he turned the radio to a jazz station and watched as Desiree leaned back in her seat and closed her eyes.

***

Geoffrey fell asleep halfway through *Zombie Strippers* and was startled awake by a knock on the door. Uncle Brew answered it and was telling whoever it was, to come back later.

"It's okay," the director shouted. "Who is it?"

He hoped it was Rebecca.

"It's Sewer Jack and some chick," the comedian replied.

"That's Sewer Rat," the singer/actor said as he pushed his way into the room. It wasn't Rebecca that followed him, however, but Barbara Quincy.

Well, he thought, at least I can stare at a real set of knockers instead of those on TV.

Sewer Rat carried his old, beat-up acoustic guitar.

"We thought you might be getting bored," Barbara said. "We

114

sat down and wrote a new song. It's called 'Loving a Zombie Just Stinks'. Maybe it'll cheer you up."

"Maybe it would be quicker if you just pulled my plug," the director said.

"Uh?" Barbara said, confused by the remark, but Uncle Brew laughed.

Sewer Rat started strumming the guitar and Barbara sang.

> "Dating a zombie is weird
> It's even much worse than you feared
> When you kiss him on a date
> You taste a neighbor he just ate
> Yes, loving a zombie is weird.
>
> Dining with a zombie's not easy
> It can make you feel faint and quite queasy
> 'Cause when you take him out to lunch
> It's the cook he'll try to munch
> Yes, loving a zombie's not easy.
>
> Yes, my boyfriend's a zombie
> He's a dead, decaying ghoul.
> He smells of day-old garbage
> When he suntans by the pool.
> He looks at you so lovingly
> But then you see the drool.
> And it's eerie when he never talks or blinks.
> Yes, loving a zombie just stinks.
>
> To marry a zombie is scary
> The reception that you throw can be quite hairy
> 'Cause it's really not okay
> When your friends are his buffet
> Yes, loving a zombie is scary.
>
> Loving a zombie is icky
> Sex seems like it's always a quickie
> And you're afraid that you might find

115

Certain parts he left behind
Yes, loving a zombie is icky.

Yes, my boyfriend's a zombie
He's a dead, decaying ghoul.
He smells of day-old garbage
When he suntans by the pool.
He looks at you so lovingly
But then you see the drool.
And it's eerie when he never talks or blinks.
Yes, loving a zombie just stinks."

The comedian couldn't resist once they had finished. "You guys are just like Peter, Paul and Mary, but without a Peter."

"What? Now you're gonna start with the dick jokes?" Sewer Rat asked.

"Of course," the comedian replied. "If you're dying on stage you have to bring 'em back home with sex and four-letter words."

"I actually like the song a lot," Terronez said. "We gotta get you guys into a studio and record that. I think it would make a great tune to play over the end credits."

"Hey," Uncle Brew interrupted. "I got a great song about a girl with three tits."

Geoffrey rolled his eyes and pretended to go back to sleep.

***

Greg Dane pounded on Zach Wawrzyniak's door until the baldheaded reporter opened it. He had a can of beer in one hand, a cigarette in the other and *TMZ* blaring in the background.

"Hey, Snoop. What's up. Want a beer? It's warm, but it's still better than cat piss."

"No, thanks," Dane replied. "I just wondered if you'd seen Aimee Breeze recently?"

"I haven't seen her since that red carpet fiasco in L.A. You mean she's here in Angel Falls?"

"Ya, she's here. Doing a story on Terronez. Or Desiree Starr. Or, hell, who knows with her? Trouble is I haven't been able to find her."

"Well, brother, it's not hard for you to lose a girl seeing as how

116

you can't see over the rest of the crowd," Zach said with a laugh.

"Ha, ha," Dane replied.

"Hey, now that you mention it, I saw another member of the paparazzi crew come in by cab last night. Do we have convention going on here, or does it mean that there's possibly a real story here?"

Dane shrugged.

"Anyway," Zach said. "I haven't seen her, but if I do, I'll let her know you were looking for her. Meanwhile, guess I'd better get sobered up and get to work before every media outlet in the country has this story while I'm chugging warm beer and wearing out titty magazines."

Dane nodded and walked away from the room as Zach closed the door.

So, should I look for Aimee or for Desiree or is there something else going on here? he wondered.

And there certainly was something else going on at Angel Falls University. He found that out a moment later when what looked like an Aztec Queen (sans clothing) walked out of the shadows. She lifted him up as easily as a weightlifter would have lifted a 200-pound set of weights. It made it very easy for her to sink her teeth into his neck.

***

Mick pulled the Viper into the House on the Hill driveway, killed the headlights and turned off the car.

"Sorry we didn't have a better evening," he said. "Looks like Lucky Lou was a lot luckier than me tonight."

"Well, look at it this way," she said. "I'll take a nice long shower and settle back to take a look at your book."

"Yikes," he said. "That's sort of scary. Well, you are reading my book, I mean. Not the shower. Unless you have flashbacks of the Psycho shower scene like I do."

She laughed and gave him a quick kiss. Then another. And another, each kiss becomes longer and more passionate.

"Well," she finally said taking a deep breath. "I guess you could scrub my back while I take that shower."

He grinned and they both hurried inside, but the shower had to wait until they finished their repeat performance of the night at

The Cove. An hour later they showered and by the time Mick was finished toweling off, Desiree had already settled in on the couch and was reading the manuscript of *Die Laughing*.

Mick, wearing only a towel around his waist, pushed his still damp hair out of his eyes.

"You really don't have to read that now," he said, feeling a little self-conscious.

She shrugged. "I want to."

"Well," he said. "As long as it doesn't put you to sleep. And speaking of sleep, I guess I'd better hit the road. Tomorrow's another workday."

"Why don't you stay the night," Desiree suggested. "I think Rio snuck off to Orlando with some of the other crew. She wasn't here last night, and I haven't seen her all day."

"Well, it would save me that long drive home," he said.

She laughed; her mood much improved. "Right. That two-mile drive is a real killer, isn't it?"

He grinned and gave her another kiss. She reached around and jerked off his towel. "Whoops," she said. "Sorry."

"Hope you don't mind if I sleep in the nude," he whispered.

"Who said anything about sleeping?" she replied as she sat the manuscript on the side table and pulled him down toward her.

***

Donald Becker settled in on the roof of the building directly across from the House on the Hill, well hidden behind a huge air-conditioning unit. He had watched his ex-girlfriend enter the House on the Hill earlier in the evening with her new boyfriend and the dentist was furious.

"I'm twice as young, more handsome, have more money and much better in bed," he whispered to the irritating insects who were providing his only company for the evening. "And, of course, I have much better teeth."

He smiled. This is gonna be easier than I thought.

No one even knew the dentist had even left L. A. Not wanting to take a plane as that would have left a trail for the police to follow, he had driven for nearly straight 40 hours with very little sleep.

Desiree would come back to him. He knew it. Crying and despondent and eventually crawling back into his bed.

He pulled the high-powered rifle from its canvas case and adjusted the scope as he aimed the weapon at the bedroom window. He gritted his teeth when he spotted the man in her room wearing nothing but a towel around his waist. And when the towel dropped, Donald Becker nearly bit his tongue off.

His finger jerked on the trigger and the window of the dorm room shattered. Donald brushed the sweat out of his eyes so he could see through the scope again, but a noise off to his left startled him.

"What the…?"

Was she an extra for the film? And what the heck was she doing on the roof at this time of night? She looked like Aztec queen or something except she was totally naked. But when she revealed a pair of glistening fangs, Donald jerked the rifle around and took aim.

He didn't have a chance to pull the trigger before she pounced on him. Donald screamed as she sank those fangs into his neck, but strangely enough, his final thought was "what a nice set of teeth she has."

***

The window in Desiree 's dorm room shattered, and she screamed. Mick grabbed her and pulled her to the floor.

"What the hell happened?" she asked.

"Someone just shot at us," Mick replied.

"What? You're not serious."

"Serious as almost being a corpse," he said. "Stay here. I'm going to check it out," he said pulling on his jeans as he tried to stay below the window line.

"To hell with that," she said. "I'm going too."

"Too dangerous," he said. "I spent four years in the Marines, Des. Let me take care of this."

"But people should never separate, Mick. I've done enough horror movies to know that's the number one rule."

"This isn't a horror movie," Mick replied as he zipped up his pants.

"Fine," she replied. "But talk to me on your cell while you're downplaying detective."

"Sure," he replied and dialed her number as he left the room

119

and headed down the single flight of stairs. She answered on the first ring.

"I'm downstairs," he said. "I'm going outside." He was silent for some time. "I've covered a lot of ground but haven't found anything. I'm heading towards the science building, but it's too quiet out here. Maybe you should hang up and call 911."

She started to object but was cut short when Mick began cussing. "Shit!"

"Mick. Mick! What is it?"

He laughed nervously. "Nothing. I just tripped over a stupid pick axe some worker left out here."

"I think they've been working on a new swimming pool or something," she told him.

"Well, they should put their tools away at night," he said. "I almost broke my neck."

"Come on back, Mick. Please?"

"Okay," he said. "Just let me—"

"Mick?"

He spoke, but it didn't sound like he was directing the conversation into the phone. "What the—? Who the heck are you?"

And the phone went dead.

□

"We can't ignore when death draws near.
The cries, the groans, the screams we hear.
We can't ignore the taste of fear.
With one last breath,
We meet our death,
And no one sheds a tear."
-*Stan Swanson*

XIV

Zyana

(Part Three)

Death & Resurrection

"The gods have surely blessed us." Zyana fell to her knees the moment the pool of water came into view. Her three remaining acolytes duplicated her supplication to the sandy ground surrounding the clearing.

Noctalyc, however, glanced around warily.

"Something is not right," he whispered.

Zyana looked up.

"But this is surely the place," she said. I can feel the power. See how the water cascades over the rocks and splashes down into the pool like the wings of a god? This must be the water of everlasting youth we have been seeking."

"That is not what I mean," the priest whispered. His eyes moved around the glen carefully, searching through the tropical foliage of this place the Spaniards called La Florida for shadows that did not fit. Was Xolotl waiting for them? Was this truly a gateway to the levels of Hell and not the healing waters of life they sought? Did demons lurk in the darkness?

Their party was now down to three acolytes and two slaves who had carried their last remaining chest of treasure to this spot. The journey had taken them nearly a year and cost them nearly every chest of treasure they had carried along the way.

Zyana rose slowly to her feet, her senses beginning to tingle.

"Apparently, the gods have not blessed us after all," she said. "Why do they play these games with us?"

She did not even attempt to draw the jeweled dagger from her sash as nearly 30 Spanish conquistadors dressed in metal armor stepped from the evergreens that grew in this part of La Florida. Many soldiers had muskets pointed in their direction while others had swords drawn and ready at their sides.

Zyana cursed.

She watched, not twitching a muscle as one of the Spaniards strode forth to meet them. She had learned enough Spanish when Cortez had initially occupied their capital city to understand that this man was demanding their surrender.

"You are the Juan Ponce de Leon that we have heard of?" she asked. "The one that seeks the so-called Fountain of Life?"

He shook his head and removed his feathered helmet. He didn't even try to keep his eyes from examining her well-developed form.

I should drive my dagger into his heart and show them the true strength and bravery of an Aztec warrior, she thought to herself.

The priest put a hand on her shoulder as if he knew what she was thinking or perhaps to even hold her back.

"No," the man replied. "I am Capitan Luis Portillo. At your service. I am surprised that you know the name of Ponce de Leon."

"Why is that?" Zyana said with venom in her voice. "You do not believe the Aztec have the intelligence to know what is going on in the world?"

He smiled. "Ah, I thought you were of the Aztec people. You are far from home."

Zyana returned the smile. "So are you, Capitan Portillo."

He laughed. "Very good. Now, we must discuss the apparent problem we have regarding this land and your act of trespassing."

"You lay claim to this land?" Zyana asked.

"Ah, my beautiful new friend. Espana lays claim not just to this land, but to the world," he said. "And, yes, that includes this insignificant pool you have come across. Now, I am not a violent man. Would you like to join us for our feast of discovery before we allow you to leave this place for the glory of Spain?"

"I would rather drink from your skull," Zyana spat.

The Spaniard was somewhat surprised by her response and a little more than annoyed, but he tried not to reveal it. He was not very successful.

"So you would rather be enemies than friends?" he finally said.

"We are already enemies," she countered. "Your conquistador allies already destroyed my city and killed thousands just to try and put my people in their place."

"Ah," he replied. "But that is in the past. You should accept that Espana is your conqueror and move on. Why hold grudges, beautiful one?"

"Do I look like someone who has been conquered?" she demanded.

He smiled. "Perhaps not, but maybe I will have that opportunity later." He turned to his men. "Seize them," he commanded.

A handful of his troops surrounded Zyana and her small group with no resistance. Noctalyc could tell that Zyana could barely constrain herself from fighting back, especially when one of the troops jerked her dagger from its sheath.

"Now," Portillo said. "The invitation to dine with us still stands. But first we must test the magical powers of the fountain."

Portillo strode forward toward the pool, removing his heavy armor as he went. He stopped at the edge of the water and smiled.

"It is somewhat ironic that I, Luis Portillo, should be the first to discover this fountain of youth," he said. "It is I who will go down in history and not Ponce de Leon. I never did like the man. Much too civilized for my taste."

He laughed and stepped forward, wading into the water. His laughter grew with each step further into the pool. He waded forward until he was near the cascading water fall that streamed over the red rocks of the small cliff behind it. The water level reached mid-chest and he splashed in it like some small child.

Then he stepped forward to stand beneath the waterfall itself.

The laughter suddenly stopped as the water streaming down over the rock outcropping turned red. Then suddenly, the man screamed and began tearing at his clothes as he struggled to wade back to the bank of the pool. He was nearly there when the skin began to melt from his body. Those near the edge of the water stepped away as his face seemed to melt and simply slide away from his gleaming skull.

He fell forward at the edge of the pool which was now a crimson red in color. He reached out, but all that touched the sand was the skeletal remains of his hand. The screaming had stopped long ago.

Zyana, who was the only person not to back away from the pool, laughed.

Perhaps the gods were on her side after all.

Maybe she and her small group were outnumbered, but if this had any chance of surviving, now was the time.

She turned. "Spanish pigs! Perhaps you should have more than one god to protect you. Where is he now? Hear what I say and bow down before me. I am Zyana, Queen of the Aztecs."

But the Spaniards did not agree with her.

"She is a demon," one of them shouted. "She has used her powers of witchcraft to kill the Capitan. Destroy her!"

A dozen muskets fired at the same moment.

A quizzical look filled Zyana's face as she felt blood flowing from her wounds.

"But I am Zyana," she whispered. "I am Queen of the Aztecs."

Her bright eyes dimmed, and she fell forward, lifeless in the sandy dirt.

***

Noctalyc kneeled beside the body of Zyana, tears rolling down his cheeks.

One of the Spaniards, apparently the second-in-command, stepped forward. His eyes were not on the woman, but rather on the skeletal remains of Capitan Portillo's hand and fingers.

"Madre de Dios," he said in a low tone. "This evil witch has turned the magical Fountain of Youth into a fountain of death. A fountain of blood . . . "

His gaze finally turned to rest upon the body of the Aztec

woman.

"She must be destroyed!" he said, his voice growing louder. "Throw her into the bloody waters and let the evil eat her body as well."

The murmurings of his troops swelled in agreement and several men stepped forward. They picked up her lifeless body and tossed it into the pool. It floated for a few seconds and then disappeared from view.

The man then turned to the priest.

"And," he said. "I would like for you and your companions to join her."

Noctalyc's face remained passive, the traces of his tears winding down his weathered and dusty face. He stood and lifted his face to the skies, mumbling words of prayer as he stepped forward toward the blood-red water.

But as he raised a foot to wade into the pool, something stirred in the water.

A moment later a head rose from the center of the pool. It wasn't a skull, it was a head, its long dark hair streaming with droplets of blood. The figure moved forward through the water, firm naked breasts appearing next then the rest of her unclothed body as she almost glided through the pool towards the sandy beach. The blood-red water flowed down over her breasts and then down her hips and legs. The acidic water had eaten away her clothing, but her flesh was soft, gleaming in the pale light of the moon.

As she stepped from the pool, her eyes changed slowly from brown to a bright red.

"I am Zyana, Queen of the Aztecs," she said.

The Capitan drew his sword and drove it deep into her stomach. He then stepped back and withdrew it, expecting her to fall once again. She simply smiled and put a bloody finger to her lips. When she smiled she revealed gleaming white fangs.

A moment later her mouth was around the Spaniard's throat, the fangs digging deep into his jugular. Another moment and his pale lifeless body dropped to the sand. Then she seemed to disappear in a whirlwind of motion. The next time she stood still, the bodies of two dozen Spaniards lay in the blood-soaked sand

and dirt.

Only Noctalyc and the two remaining acolytes remained alive. The priest had not moved or even shown the slightest reaction to what had just occurred.

Zyana stepped forward, covered in blood that was not her own and bowed before the priest.

"For the glory of the gods and the dawn of a new Mexicana," she said. "The Aztec reign begins once more. It will rise from the dead. Just like its queen."

She smiled and Noctalyc saddened at the sight of her gleaming fangs which were now covered with blood. Another stream of tears rolled down his cheeks. But they were not tears of joy.

"It cannot be this way, my daughter," he whispered. "I feared the legends might be true. Eternal youth? Yes. Eternal life? Yes. But only to the dead. It is blasphemy and an insult to the gods."

Zyana's eyes blazed.

"How dare you speak to me in that manner," she screamed. "I am your Queen!"

"This is not the will of the gods . . . "

She hissed. "I still thirst, Noctalyc. Do you desire to change your views, or shall I have a taste of your blood?"

"I am sorry, my daughter."

He pulled a small box from his robe and handed it to Zyana.

"What is this?" she asked, her red eyes blazing.

He shrugged. "A small gift before you send me to the gods."

She lifted the lid and at first saw nothing in the black cloth lining of the box. Then a small red spider scuttled out and leapt to her arm. She laughed and swatted it away into the sand.

"A gift? You call this a gift?"

"It is a gift to the gods," he replied. "A gift to the Mexica people."

She laughed and brought a foot down to squash the small creature. She felt its insignificant bite as she ground it into the ground.

"And to think I once called you father," she said. "But now I thirst."

She reached down to grab him, but then winced. And soon her face twisted in painful anguish.

"What have you done!" she screamed.

The spider venom acted quickly, speeding through her body.

And one more time, she toppled to the earth. His heart still beat, but she was paralyzed by the toxic venom.

***

It took Noctalyc and his acolytes weeks to carve the sarcophagus.

Then they dug deep into the soft ground.

The priest draped her body in simple white cloth and arranged the last few pieces of their remaining treasure on her body. A necklace, a headband, and golden bracelets.

He also placed a dozen red spiders into the sarcophagus with her inert body.

"Feast well," he told the creatures. "The Queen needs her sleep and only you can give it to her."

Noctalyc muttered a prayer as the acolytes closed the lid of her burial container and wound it with chains. He carefully added locks to the chains, then tossed the keys into the pool of blood.

Once the dirt had been replaced, Noctalyc motioned for the acolytes to leave him in peace. When they were gone, he knelt before her grave and said a last prayer to the gods.

He then spoke to his daughter's resting place.

"Sleep peacefully, my child," he said.

He then took the knife she had carried with her for years and slid it slowly across his throat.

"Long live Zyana, Queen of the Aztecs," he whispered with his last breath. "Hopefully she will sleep forever. The world will surely be damned if she does not...."

""I cannot stop the hooves that pound
As death rides on his steed.
I can't ignore the gleaming blade
It's all but guaranteed.

Little do I know of death
Or what's beyond the veil.
But ignorance is never bliss
As death will still prevail."
-*Stan Swanson*

XV
College of the Living Dead

Desiree grabbed her black panties and t-shirt from the floor and slipped them along with a pair of running shoes. At the last moment, she grabbed the combination penlight/pepper spray from her purse. Cell phone in hand, she bounded down the stairs two steps at a time and considered herself lucky she hadn't sprained an ankle or broken a leg.

She ran across the courtyard and stopped. The penlight was of little use as she looked around in desperation, but it was better than nothing.

"Mick?" she yelled.

Then she remembered him saying something about tripping over a pickaxe and headed towards the area where the new swimming pool was being constructed near the university president's on-campus home. It was dark and she nearly tripped over the same pickaxe, but at least she knew she was headed in the right direction. She picked up the axe. One of the ends was long and pointed, the other shorter, almost like the end of a hoe, but much larger and sharper. It looked as if it could cut through a chunk of steel. She didn't know if she would be able to use it when the time came, but it made her feel better.

She glanced around. From where she stood, she figured Mick would have either headed back downhill towards the Slough Path and the woods or the old Bell Tower which loomed off to her right. She debated flipping a coin, but she really didn't want to venture into the woods around the bog anyway.

There might be gators in there, she thought, or gator-people or who knows what.

"Mick!" she called out again, but there was no answer except for her distant echo off the campus buildings. The Bell Tower was foreboding, but she figured it was the lesser of two evils. Likely no gators or snakes in there...

She ran up the path, unconcerned about running around in her panties and no bra under the T-shirt and stopped in front of the tower. There had been a lock on the door when she had first arrived on campus. She had remembered it during her brief tour of the university.

There was no lock on the door now.

In fact, it stood wide open, almost begging her to enter.

She took a deep breath, thought about all the horror movies she had been in and watched over the years, but stepped inside anyway. Her concern for Mick was greater than her fear.

The penlight was nearly useless, but moonlight streamed in from somewhere near the top of the tower. An old wooden spiral staircase ran around the circular walls of the tower and seemed to stretch upward into heaven. Or maybe hell, she thought.

"Mick? Hello? Is anyone there?"

She went up the stairs very cautiously, the wooden steps creaking menacingly with each step she took. It was very easy to picture the staircase giving way and her falling to what would hopefully be a quick and painless death. She reached the top, but only found a giant silver bell. She looked out over the balcony, got dizzy and stepped back quickly.

Desiree wiped a single tear away from her face, which was now layered in dust and slowly headed back down the stairs. One of the wooden steps broke and she reached out and caught the railing in the wall just in time. Even the railing felt like it would pull loose at any moment. She stepped over the broken step and hurried to the bottom, no longer concerned about safety. She just wanted out of the dark tower.

She stepped outside and took a deep breath of the fresh air, a welcome change from the stale fetid smell inside the tower.

Desiree thought for a moment, then realized she was still holding her cell phone. She quickly punched in Mick's number and heard the ringtone she had downloaded yesterday. It was the Doors' "Hello, I Love You." She held her own cell phone away from her ear and listened closely. She could hear the song coming from a different location. The location of his phone!

But he didn't answer. She hit 'End' before the phone went to voice mail. She didn't want the sound of his recorded voice to be the last time she heard it. Besides, she needed to dial again to pinpoint the phone's location.

It was coming from inside the bell tower.

She scowled and stepped slowly back into the dark shadows of the building.

The tune was coming from below.

She shined the thin beam from her penlight and discovered a wooden trap door behind the staircase. There was a lower level to the structure. This fact cheered her up and frightened her at the same time. Would she find Mick's lifeless body below? Or simply his Cell phone?

Desiree opened the trap door. It was clear most of the dust that should have accumulated around it, but there were clearly footprints in the dust and dirt that remained. A ladder led down into the darkness. She rang his number again, and it was louder and coming from the underground part of the tower. She took a deep breath and started down the ladder.

The subterranean room was huge and spider webs were spun from one corner to the other, but they were different from most spider webs she had seen. These were larger and thicker and the silky pockets over the maze of webs held victims, but they were not flies and insects. There were people. Bodies.

Desiree nearly screamed, but her emotions were so drained, it was like she didn't have the energy to do even that. He first thought was that perhaps this was one of Geoffrey's elaborate sets. But when she lifted the penlight to the webbing, she saw a face she recognized as Michelangelo DeSalvo. Except the face was withered and the skin was dry, like he had aged a hundred years overnight.

The corpse (and there was little doubt it was a corpse) was an empty husk of a body, almost as if it had been sucked completely dry of blood and body fluids.

"Help me," a voice said softly.

The voice reminded her of the old '50s movie, *The Fly*, when a tiny human's head was attached to the body of a fly and trapped in the silken spider web.

She aimed her penlight in the direction of the voice and recognized Roland Bannister, the university president. He was tightly bound in the webbing and hanging from the rafters of the underground lair.

"What the—"

"Please. Help me out before she comes back!"

"Before whom comes back?" Desiree asked desperately. "Have you seen Mick?"

"I don't know any frigging Mick," Bannister snapped, some strength returning to his voice. "I've been here since yesterday. Now get me the hell out of here before she comes back."

"Mick Collins," she said, nearly oblivious to the man's plight as he hung there upside down in the webbing. "He works for you in the facilities department."

"Get me down!" he spat. "Get me down and I'll help you find him!"

Knowing it was better to have another person with her, she grabbed at the sticky webbing and pulled strands of it away until the man slipped out and fell hard to the floor.

"Sorry," she whispered.

He wasn't very appreciative of her help. "Crazy bitch."

"Whatever," she snapped in return. "Now help me find my boyfriend."

"Find him yourself," he said. "I'm getting the hell out of here.

I'd advise you to do the same thing before that spider lady comes back. You won't stand a chance, missy."

"Spider lady?" she whispered, but before she could utter another word, the university president had scrambled up the ladder and was gone.

She heard another muffled voice and changed the direction of the beam from her penlight. It was Greg Dane and just like Roland Bannister, he was covered from head to toe in the webbing. He moved and it sounded like he was half trying to say something and half crying. A gob of webbing covered most of his mouth.

Desiree quickly peeled away the layers of webbing and this time helped the victim down before he fell straight to the floor.

"Oh, God, thank you," he gasped. "I was so afraid I was going to be next."

"Next?" Desiree asked.

"She is like some giant spider except she looks like a woman, but she can crawl along the walls and hang from the ceiling and spin these webs and has long fangs which she uses to suck out your blood and she—"

She put a hand on his arm which was still wrapped in sticky webbing. "Slow down, Greg. You're rambling. I can barely keep up."

"You saw what she did to Michelangelo. She's done it to others too. I think it keeps her alive. She comes back to feed and then goes back to her digging."

"Digging?" the Scream Queen asked.

She's digging tunnels or something. Like she's searching for something. She's like some crazy human-spider-vampire-mole lady. Wears nothing more than some fancy Aztec jewelry. We need to go. It's almost feeding time and I don't want to be the next meal."

"No!" Desiree said sharply. "I have to find Mick."

"Tall? Dark hair? Only wearing a pair of jeans?"

"Yes," she replied, the excitement clear in her voice.

"I think she brought him in earlier. I think he's in back. Sorry, but not sure she hasn't already killed him, hon. She was back there draining someone, so it was either him or your old boyfriend."

"My old boyfriend?"

"Yeah. That dentist guy you use to date."

"Donald Becker is here? Why...?"

Greg's face was white as an old tombstone, and she watched him sink weakly to the floor. She knew he wouldn't be any help. Pickaxe in one hand and cell phone and penlight in the other, she moved slowly around towards the back of the room.

It was like the catacombs from some old black and white movie. She pushed strands of webbing away from her face and spit some out. It was everywhere.

She found Donald Becker first. His eyes were wide open in death and his body seemed an empty shell of his former self. The only thing that still seemed perfect in the dim light were his teeth. Under different circumstances, Desiree might have found it humorous.

"I have the need," Donald said spitting out blood and gore out of his mouth. "The need for speed."

Then silence.

She could tell by the dead look in his eyes, that he had passed away.

Desiree was choked, even though he was an ex-boyfriend, she hated to see anybody die such a horrible death. Then she remembers what her ex just said, and said, "wasn't that a quote from a Tom Cruise movie?"

Of course, the corpse didn't respond.

***

"Des ..."

The Scream Queen jumped, thinking the voice had come from the obviously dead Donald Becker. Then she realized that the body hanging next to him, tightly wrapped in fresh webbing, was Mick Collins.

"Oh, God, Mick. You had me scared to death."

"Don't say that word," he said.

"What word? Death?"

His laugh was strained. "Yeah, that's the one."

She reached out to tear the webbing away from him, but he yelled just in time. "Des! Behind you!"

Desiree spun around and there stood the spider lady everyone had been talking about. The Scream Queen and the creature stood

133

there staring at each other, neither moving.

And then Desiree heard a voice. But the voice was in her head.

"I am Zyana, Queen of the Aztecs."

Desiree shook her head, but the voice continued to invade her mind. "Do you have what I seek?"

"Wh... what do you seek?" Desiree asked, her voice seeming exceedingly loud in the room.

"I am Zyana, Queen of the Aztecs. Do you have what I seek? Do you know where the Fountain of Blood flows?"

"Aztec? The...the Aztecs are dead and long gone," Desiree whispered.

"You lie!"

Desiree shook her head.

"I am queen! I command you to answer my question. Where is it?"

Desiree sighed and couldn't resist. It had, after all, been a very long week. "Have you tried looking up your ass?"

Rage filled the spider lady's face, and she scrambled forward, baring her long fangs. Without thinking, Desiree lifted the pickaxe and bit deeply into the monster's shoulder. The scream was what Desiree would later describe as a mixture of a wild banshee and a cat in heat. Zyana grabbed at the edge of the hole she had dug, but then slipped and fell backwards into the pit.

Desiree dropped the pickaxe, now covered with purple-colored blood, and began ripping the webs away from Mitch.

"Hurry!" he said, but he hardly had to remind her as they both heard movement at the bottom of the tunnel.

The sound grew closer. Maybe the creature was wounded, but she was certainly not down and out for the count.

"Go, Des. Before it's too late--" the facility man said.

"No way," she spat. "One dead boyfriend hanging around here is enough."

"Boyfriend?"

"Ex-boyfriend," she added.

She heard the screams of the desperate and very angry creature scrambling up the tunnel wall; the sounds were getting louder and closer.

Desiree pulled with every ounce of strength she had and finally the webbing broke and Mick tumbled to the ground, forcing all the air from his lungs. He gasped for breath that wouldn't come as Desiree half pulled and half carried him up the ladder. She was reminded of mothers who had pulled cars off the top of their kids.

Not knowing which direction to run, Desiree helped Mick down the path. The nearest building was the university president's house. Perhaps the idiot hadn't helped her before, but it was still the closest thing to a place to hide.

They had just reached the edge of the half-finished swimming pool at the edge of Roland Bannister's property when Zyana crashed through the bushes and blocked their path. It seemed as if the wound in her shoulder was already healing. The vampire/spider/Aztec queen almost seemed to smile as she bared her very sharp and many teeth.

Mick, having regained his breath and feeling very protective, pushed Desiree behind him.

"Come on, bitch," he spat at the creature. "Give me all you got."

But he got more than he was expecting. She didn't attack. She simply held out her fingers and strands of web shot out and wound around him, leaving him once again helpless.

"Damn it --Aztec piece of crap," Des shouted. "You're not gonna kill another one of my boyfriends. This one's a keeper." She glanced around and saw the chainsaw sitting on a nearby sawhorse. It was gas-powered and she was glad she had spent summers helping her dad clear dead trees and brush in their backyard when she was younger.

She fired up the chainsaw and swung it in a wide arc. Zyana, having no idea what the implement was, simply raised her arm which Desiree immediately cut off at the elbow.

The vampire queen was stunned and as she gazed at the stump of her arm, Desiree swung the chainsaw once more and Zyana's head simply rolled off the shoulders of her body and into the unfinished hole that was supposed to eventually be a swimming pool. Her body wobbled crazily for a moment, then toppled after her head.

But just as relief flooded Desiree 's body and she shut off the chainsaw, she saw Zyana's head fluttering its eyelids and her headless body begin crawling up the side of the hole. Desiree thanked her personal trainer for all those years of exercise and martial arts and, with a perfect roundhouse kick, the body went flying back into the hole.

Mick glanced around and winked at Desiree.

"Be right back," he said and ran for the truck loaded with bags of cement ready to be mixed and poured the next day. Desiree had to continue kicking the obstinate body of the spider lady several times before Mick had backed up the truck and dumped dozens of 80-pound cement bags into the hole, quickly covering the body and head of their attacker.

Moments later they stood with hose in hand and slowly watched the pool fill and begin soaking into the bags.

He leaned over and kissed her.

"They can add some more Quikcrete and smooth it over in the morning," he said. "I think it will make a great tennis court."

She laughed and returned the kiss.

"College of the Living Dead," she whispered.

"What?" he asked.

"Nothing," she said and sank deep into his arms as the morning sun rose over the bog to the east.

One Year Later:

Desiree Geoffrey Terronez

Terronez was arrested immediately upon the discovery of the dead bodies in the bell tower underground lair. He was the prime suspect in the deaths until officials simply had to believe the story that Aimee Breeze, Greg Dane, Rio Ruiz, Desiree Starr and Mick Collins spun. The authorities didn't believe the tale for a second, but without further proof, they knew the charges would never stick. With all of the publicity (and the fact that it was simply a damned good horror movie), *College of the Living Dead* was a runaway hit pulling in twice the money of Hell's Bells. It opened at the number two spot. A half-plotted comedy with Tom Cruise and Scarlet Johansson was number one. Thinking of the future, he put any plans for movie making on hold. He stayed in Angel Falls, moved in with Rebecca Morton and they tried their hand at writing screenplays.

Roland Bannister

Bannister was never heard from again. The safe in his office was empty and gossip had it that he had fled with over two million dollars in cash. It was rumored he was last seen in Argentina.

Paul Doonan

With Roland Bannister out of the picture, Angel Falls University promoted him to president. The news about the Bell Tower and what supposedly went on there was nothing but good news for the college. Despite many a parent's dismay, the enrollment of the college for the New Year was the largest in the history of the school. The running joke was that AFU now stood for All Freaks University.

Rebecca Morton

Rebecca was promoted to Vice President of Enrollment, Communication and Planning when Doonan became the President. She kept her position as Director of Marketing s well and received a healthy raise and bonus. She really didn't need the money as she spent all of her time at work, writing screenplays with her new partner, Geoffrey Terronez, and spending lots of time in bed with him.

Lucreita Terronez

Exhausted after making *College of the Living Dead* and handling most of the special effects, co-directing, co-producing and even some acting and stunts for the film, she took some time off and spent several months Ireland with her musician boyfriend Sewer Rat. She knew it was only a matter of time before she was drawn back into the business, but the time off did her a world of good.

Sewer Rat

Although *College of the Living Dead* was a big hit and more acting roles came down the pike, he decided to get out of the movie business and back into the music business. The song he and Barbara had written for the movie hit #10 on the U.S. charts. He also decided to go solo and sent the other members of the Dead Corpses on their way. Within two years he had two number one singles and was eventually knighted by the Queen. She knighted him Sir Leonard Habersham, but he preferred to be called Sir Sewer Rat, much to the Queen's dismay.

Aimee Breeze

Her live newscast from Angel Falls about the *College of the Living Dead* and the mysterious happenings on the campus made *Entertainment Right Now* ratings go through the roof. She became news anchor for the show and was soon engaged to Greg Dane. They moved in together in a house once owned by Vincent Price.

Greg Dane

The stories he filed about *College of the Living Dead* made *The National Snoop* one of the best-selling tabloids at supermarkets across the United States. When Ed Devin, editor and publisher of the tabloid, decided to retire, the job went to Snoopy. He was happy to have the extra money as the wedding Aimee put together cost him every last cent he had in the bank.

Zach Wawrzyniak

Zack's new column in *Monster Agogo Magazine* brought the publication back to life and the web version of the magazine sold thousands of online subscriptions in the first month alone. He soon became assistant editor and his luck with the scream queens and ladies of Hollywood was never better.

Barbara Quincy

Although she enjoyed making *College of the Living Dead*, Barbara decided to reunite the Bee Girls and were booked solidly for the next year at colleges and small music halls across the United States, Canada and Europe. Their biggest hit, Vampire Queens in Old Blue Jeans, was only kept from the number spot on the U. S. charts by one of Sir Sewer Rat's singles.

Gina Bellarossi

Although her major role in *College of the Living Dead* assured, she wouldn't have play small parts as a scantily-clad secretary any time soon, she decided to join her new life partner, Barbara Quincy, and became a back-up singer for the Bee Girls. She and Desiree Starr are still the best of friends.

Slim Jim Atkins

Slim Jim left his job at Angel Falls University and was elected Deputy Sheriff in the next election when Sheriff Stroud was accused of lewd public behavior with actress Rio Ruiz. He met a cashier from the local Wal-mart, they settled down and had seven kids.

Rio Ruiz

Rio stayed in Angel Falls for a few weeks until her affair with Sheriff Stroud broke off, then returned to Brazil where she became the most sought-after model of the past decade, topless or otherwise.

Uncle Brew

More movie roles, TV commercial spots and comedy gigs came rolling in after the success of *College of the Living Dead*. He recently filmed a comedy special for HBO which will air this Halloween. The special is called *Laughing All the Way to The Blood Bank*. The cast and crew of the movie had front row seats.

Dr. Joshua Franklin

Although he was on vacation during the summer and missed everything that had happened at the college, he was given full permission to examine the stone sarcophagus when Randy Bannister's truck was pulled from the bog. He wrote a book, *The Curse of The Aztec Vampire Queen*, which sold hundreds of thousands of copies.

Mick Collins

Because of all of the publicity and his role in defeating the vampire queen, he was promoted to head of facilities by the new college president. He also continued to date his movie star Scream Queen Desiree who regularly flew back and forth between Hollywood and Florida. His book, *Die Laughing*, was published and the script is now in the hands of Blake Smith and his teddy bear, Mr. Twinks.

Desiree Starr

The same critics that panned *Bullet City* were now praising Desiree for her role in *College of the Living Dead* with headlines like: "An A Plus," "Head of the class," and "Making the grade." She was even nominated for an Academy Award although everyone knew she had no chance. She finally finished *Memoirs of a Scream Queen,* which also became a bestseller. She is currently splitting her time between Hollywood and Florida where she spends most of her time with Mick Collins. They have added two more cats to the household.

ABOUT THE AUTHORS:

LINNEA QUIGLEY

Linnea Quigley is one of the world's most famous Scream Queens of all time, named as such by her fans and numerous publications across the globe (including Playboy Magazine in 2017, who named her "The sexiest scream queen of all time."). She has won numerous awards over the years for her work in film, most recently the Trailblazer Award at 2018's **Idaho Horror Film Festival**. Linnea is a fan favorite at horror conventions and special appearances at film screenings and horror events around the world.

Barbara Linnea Quigley was born in Davenport, Iowa to Heath and Dorothy Quigley. Her mother was a homemaker and her father a noted psychologist and chiropractor. Always a shy child, her mother encouraged her to take up gymnastics. After moving with her family to Los Angeles in the late 1970s, Linnea began working at a Jack Lalanne Spa. The beautiful ingénue was encouraged to try modeling and acting. She soon received small parts in commercials and B-movies, such as **Wheeler (1975)** and **Stone Cold Dead (1979)**. Her breakout role as Trash in **Return of the Living Dead (1985)** went on to become a cult classic and firmly established her as "Queen of the B's". Her reign is supreme with such films as **Sorority Babes in the Slimeball Bowl-O-Rama (1988) Night of the Demons (1988) Hollywood Chainsaw Hookers (1988)** and **Pumpkinhead II: Blood Wings (1993). Linnea Quigley's Horror Workout (1990)** is something dreamed up while working on a film. It became an overnight hit and still has a huge fan base. Today, fans dress as her film characters for Halloween, horror conventions, birthday parties etc.

Linnea has written two books about her life in the B-movie industry, **T*he Linnea Quigley Bio & Chainsaw Book*** and ***I'm Screaming as Fast as I Can: My Life in B-Movies*** and is about to embark on her third book. Mysticism of all kinds has always enthralled her. Linnea has conducted séances, reads tarot cards, and loves everything to do with white magic.

Linnea also is a musician. She sang and played guitar in the band The Skirts for a number of years. They recorded a few popular albums before eventually disbanding, as Linnea wanted to focus full time on her acting career, in addition to her numerous charitable causes. Music is still important in her life and she continues to write songs.

Linnea is a devoted animal rights advocate and also leads a strict vegan lifestyle. She has a dozen rescue dogs and is currently working towards building an animal sanctuary to help more animals.

After starring in more than 200 films, Linnea Quigley is and will always be *our* favorite "Scream Queen".

MICHAEL McCARTY

Michael McCarty has been a professional writer since 1983 and the author of over forty books of fiction and nonfiction, as well as hundreds of articles, short stories and poems. He is a Five-Time Bram Stoker Finalist and winner of the David R. Collins' Literary Achievement Award from the Midwest Writing Center. He is the author of such books DARK CITIES: DARK TALES, DARK DUETS: MUSICAL MAYHEM, A LITTLE HELP FROM MY FIENDS, I KISSED A GHOUL and LOST GIRL OF THE LAKE (with Joe McKinney.)

His nonfiction includes MODERN MYTHMAKERS, ESOTERIA-LAND, CONVERSATIONS WITH KRESKIN (with The Amazing Kreskin), GHOSTS OF THE QUAD CITIES (with Mark McLaughlin), EERIE QUAD CITIES (with John Brassard Jr.) and QUAD CITIES BEER: A HISTORY (with Kristin DeMarr).

His stories and interviews have appeared in a wide variety of magazines and anthologies including Fangoria, Cemetery Dance, Starlog, Filmfax, ON WRITING HORROR (A Handbook by the Horror Writers Association, edited by Mort Castle), MIDNIGHT

PREMIERE and IN LAYMON TERMS (both anthos from Cemetery Dance publications).

BITERS: TALES OF ZOMBIES & VAMPIRES is his first publication from Black Bed Sheet Books.

He lives in Rock Island, Illinois with his wife Cindy and pet rabbit Yeti.

STAN SWANSON

Stan Swanson is the author of seven books. A longtime singer/songwriter, he has written two books on songwriting, INSPIRATION FOR SONGWRITERS (2006) and THE SONGWRITER'S JOURNAL (2007).

Also enjoying young adult literature, he wrote two fantasy novels including DRAGONTOOTH (2003) and THE MISADVENTURES OF HOBART HUCKLEBUCK (2007).

His journey into the horror genre began with FOREVER ZOMBIE, a short story collection and a highly praised nonfiction book for writers, WRITE OF THE LIVING DEAD, written with Araminta Star and Rachel Lee. And of course the horror novel, RETURN OF THE SCREAM QUEEN with Michael McCarty and Linnea Quigley.

The Authors with the Tar Man from Return of the Living Dead.

The Wizard of Ooze

by Michael McCarty & Linnea Quigley

Scottie Thomas was used to dealing with all kinds of Hollywood slime-ball types. He'd seen them all over the years. The sleazy producers who wanted to sleep with the stars, male or female — or robotic, if it was a sci-fi epic. The diva writers who threw hissy-fits if an actor changed even one precious word of their screenplays. The egomaniacal actors who wouldn't budge an inch out of their doublewide luxury trailers until everything went completely their way.

Normally Scottie was able to project a nonchalant manner — but sitting outside of the windowless office door stenciled 'Jeffrey Terronez: Special-Effects God' had him sweating like a crack addict and made his heart pound like he'd just run the Boston Marathon. He felt like he was waiting forever, but actually it had only been twenty minutes.

In his career, Scottie had worked with some of the crème de la crème of special-effects artists — Rick Baker, Stan Winston, Steve Johnston, Rob Bottin and Tom Savini. He had always wanted to do a film with Terronez, who had made a cottage industry for himself for his realistic gore effects, earning him the nickname "The Wizard of Ooze."

The petite blonde secretary had popped into Terronez' office five minutes earlier, and now the door opened and she slipped back into the waiting area. She didn't even look at Scottie as she trotted on her stiletto heels back to her desk. She wore dark sunglasses, a white mini-skirt and a tight white pullover that showed off a bosom that was more implants than flesh. "What was your name again?" she asked, popping her bubble gum between *your* and *name*.

"Scottie Thomas, director of—"

She tapped a button on her intercom with a long red fingernail. "Some director guy named Scottie Thomas wants to see you."

There was a moment of silence. Then a voice on the other end finally said, "Send him in."

***

The first thing Scottie noticed was the office's minimal decor. There was only four pieces of furnishing in the whole place – a massive white oak desk with a white chair behind it and another one in front of it, and a white turntable console.

Who had record players in this age?

The soft, slightly crackling strains of Bach's "Ave Marie" played softly in the background.

Everything in the room was immaculately hospital-white: the walls and ceiling, the shag carpet and thick curtains, even the rug-runner leading up to the desk.

Jeffrey was dressed in white silky pajamas and stood at the window, looking out over the city. All Scottie could see was his back and his long, long flowing black hair.

"Have a seat," the special-effects man said. The director did as he was told.

Jeffrey turned around. He wore a pair of black horn-rimmed sunglasses. *PJs and shades? Pretty weird outfit for three in the afternoon – even by Hollywood standards,* Scottie thought.

"Why did you come here and interrupt my transcendental meditation?" Jeffrey asked.

"I have a movie–"

"Ahhh," he said, clasping his hands together. "Another script. Everyone seems to have a script for me to read. Every busboy, bartender and taxi driver and golf caddy. Even my secretary, and she only types sixteen words a minute. Go on."

"My producer, Jerry Buckingham the third, has a generous offer if you want to do the film…" the director said, handing him a slip of paper with a figure written on it.

Jeffrey took a look at the paper and sneered. "I don't care about your chicken feed."

"We have a great script, written by hot new screenwriters Kevin Weston and Josh Yuspa," he said. He set the script on the desk.

"I don't care about your soporific screenplay," the special-effects guru said with a dismissive wave of his hand.

Scottie started to sweat more. "We have Lisa England, star of

146

Attack of the Giant Leeches from Outer Space, and Danny Carpenter, star of the cable-TV series *Vampires of Vegas.*"

"I don't care about your has-beens and wannabes."

Scottie paused and thought about the situation. "What *do* you care about, then?"

Jeffrey drew closer, then leaned against the desk to lower his face to Scottie's level. "Does the movie have a lot of gore? Lots and lots of stomach-churning violence? Is it bloody? Buckets of blood, blood and more blood?"

"Yes. It is filled with gruesome, gratuitous, senseless violence."

The special-effects man finally smiled. "Then I will do it." He pressed a button on the intercom. "Ermelinde, I'll be doing business with our visitor, Mr. Thomas. Please bring in the appropriate documents."

Within seconds, the busty blonde entered the office with a pile of papers that must have weighed at least twenty pounds. She dropped the bundle on the desk and strutted back to her office.

"Maybe I should have my lawyer look at all this first..." Scottie said, leafing through the papers. Some of the pages even had phrases in Old English and Latin.

"Successful working relationships are built on trust, not arguments made by debating ambulance chasers. I'm sorry I misjudged you. Obviously there is a lack of trust here and..."

Before the special-effects artist could finish his sentence, Scottie picked up his pen and said, "Where do I sign?"

Jeffrey flashed him a devilish grin. "For starters, here on page 68 at the bottom, and on page 69 on the top, and..."

***

Scottie sat in his director's chair and checked his watch for what seemed like the thousandth time. Jeffrey Terronez was three hours late. He called the special-effects man's office, cell-phone, even his pager – no answer. This was the first day of filming the effects and the director was as nervous as a man with pants covered in honey, sitting on top of a South American fire ant mound.

A bus came roaring down the road and came to a screeching halt in front of the film crew. The bus looked like the one at the end of *The Gauntlet* minus the bullet holes and Clint Eastwood. Every window was covered with a steel plate and on the side of the vehicle in big white letters was painted "The Wizard of Ooze." The bus even had vanity license plates that read, FX GOD.

Lucreita was the first to step off the bus. She was dressed in white, but it failed to make her look virginal: tight white slacks and a white tube-top that barely covered her plump implants. Her dark shades were her only item of apparel that wasn't white. She held a megaphone to her mouth and popped her bubble-gum, which sounded like a gunshot when amplified.

"Ladies and gentlemen," the secretary said. "Please give a hand to the legendary Jeffrey Terronez."

The film crew applauded and Jeffrey stepped off the bus. He still wore white satin PJs and dark sunglasses. The tall man slowly descended the steps with his hands in prayer position.

Cristopher Garton, a young redhaired gaffer, ran up to the FX expert with a notebook in his hands. When he spoke, his high-pitched voice was reminiscent of a certain cartoon mouse. "I'm such a big fan of yours, Mr. Terronez. I've seen all your films at least ten times each. You're the reason I'm involved in the film business in the first place."

Jeffrey smiled. "It is good to worship me."

"Can I please have an autograph?" Christopher said, pushing the notebook in front of the special-effects man's face.

Emerlinde stepped in front of her boss and pushed the notebook away. "No autographs allowed," she said sternly.

"No written documentation of any kind," Terronez said flatly, walking past the stunned gaffer.

***

Things have been just plain weird since Terronez made his grand entrance, Scottie thought as he played his eighth game of solitaire, waiting for the goddamn rain to stop.

All this rain – now that's weird, the director reflected. *I picked New Mexico in the summer because it hardly ever rains this time of year. Now look at it. Shit, where's my ark? All this rain has put us a whole month behind schedule. And then the crew members keep disappearing. It's like I'm on the set of some teen slasher flick.*

The first crew member to vanish had been Cristopher Garton. Of course, the fact that Terronez had refused to give out an autograph had probably upset the kid. Cristopher was a sensitive little scrub – maybe that was why he just stopped showing up for work without even saying goodbye to anyone.

Then Danny Nicks, the soundman, took off. He went out riding his motorcycle to the nearby town to pick up some beer and never returned. But who knows, maybe he met some hot biker chick and rolled off into the sunset. Danny was the kind of horndog who would do something like that.

But the oddest disappearance had been Scottie's assistant, Leesa Matheson. She had been working with him for the last ten years. She wasn't the kind to just leave without telling anyone. Of course, Terronez has been making the filming process a living hell with all his ranting and raving. Nothing was ever good enough for him. If his chicken salad had even the tiniest speck of dark meat in it, he'd throw it to the ground in front of everyone. And woe to anyone if they handed him a fizzy soft drink that had gone just a little flat. Terronez demanded fizz, and he'll splash the drink into the face of whoever had served it to him. Five or six times, that had been Leesa.

Scottie flipped over another card. The ace of spades.

Terronez has been a real pain in the ass – but at least his effects were realistic. The fake guts, hearts, brains, eyeballs and spinal columns were the slickest and ooziest Scottie had ever seen. And the synthetic goo he used for blood actually clotted if left out too long. The effects even had a bit of realistic stink to them. Some of the cast members complained about that. Lucreita dismissed their comments by saying, "The master does not stop at visual accuracy. He believes that the performers must experience all the appropriate sensory input to foster maximal dramatic responses. So there."

Terronez only came out of his bus, which was also his special-effects mobile lab, when it was time for him to do his thing, and he always brought his blonde sidekick. She shouted out all the commands through her megaphone – it was like she was directing the picture. Whenever the special-effects guru was inside the bus, Lucreita was always standing outside, like a watchdog. What the Hell was Terronez doing in there for all those hours? Surely he'd prepared most of the special effects in advance. Why would he wait until the last minute?

Jeffrey pushed the cards off the table. He was bored with the game, and with the rain, too.

It was time for a few script changes.

***

"To hell with this fucking rain," Scottie said to nobody at all as he climbed inside the cabin of his helicopter. He'd decided he would do some aerial location shots during the downpour. Maybe later he'd work in some scenes with a 'dark-and-stormy-night' kind of feel. He started the engine and the aircraft began to rise. The director had a pilot's license from a brief military stint, and that license was now invaluable, since the original studio's pilot also had recently disappeared.

The helicopter flew over Terronez's special-effects bus. Emerlinde stood guard outside the bus holding a white umbrella. He had to admit: she was one hell of a faithful employee.

Then Scottie noticed that the bus had a skylight in the middle of the roof. Unfortunately, he was too high to see anything though the glass. The rain didn't help matters.

But still ... maybe there was a way he could see what was going on in that guarded fortress on wheels.

***

Scottie's clothes were soaked, but he didn't care. He quietly climbed up the back of the bus. He figured the sound of the rain pattering on Lucreita 's umbrella would drown out any little noise he made. He crawled over to the skylight, only to discover that it was a mirror – probably a one-way mirror, so that light could still shine in. But why would anyone put a one-way mirror on top of a vehicle? That was just plain nuts.

He pushed his fingers under the edge and managed to swing it open. Terronez and Lucreita weren't so brainy after all: they'd forgotten to lock an entrance. The director climbed inside the dim interior of the bus.

What Scottie saw he jumped down to the floor shocked and nauseated him. He vomited within eight seconds of entering the vehicle, splashing the liquefied remains of a club sandwich across the bus.

Of course, the place was already such a terrible mess, his contribution didn't make it look any worse.

He had expected to see Jeffrey Terronez smoking pot or snorting coke, or maybe having sex with one of the few remaining crew members. But it was worse than that – much worst.

Scottie saw Terronez cutting off Leesa's slender, freckled arm with a machete. He also saw the remaining body parts of other members of the film crew – on tabletops, in trays, stuffed in bottles. He even saw some heads speared on sticks, which in turn were stuck in an umbrella stand.

"So you've discovered the truth," Terronez sneered as he walked over to the director. "What took you so long? I left the latch open up there – I figured you'd find your way in."

"You'll never get away with this! I'm going to call the police," Scottie said, pulling his cellphone out of his pocket – he hoped it wasn't too wet to operate.

Terronez knocked the phone onto the floor and smashed it with his foot. "Ha! It would be hard to finish the movie with your special-effects guy in prison, wouldn't it?"

Before Scottie could answer, Terronez said, "I am indispensable – but you are not."

"What are you talking about?" Scottie said nervously. "I'm the director – I'm the most important guy here."

Terronez shrugged. "I'm afraid not. Emerlinde can fill in for you. She is a lady of many talents. Sound, camera, editing, acting, directing – she can do it all. She's a genius, really, with an I.Q. of 187. She's also my sister, and I really don't like the way you'll been ogling her. That look of fear on your face right now is really priceless! In fact, I think it would be perfect for the final decapitation scene."

Before Scottie could scream, Terronez swung the machete, slicing through the director's neck. The way the head toppled off the body looked exactly like one of Tom Savini's *Friday The 13th* effects – except for the fact that this scene used a real head.

***

The Los Angeles world premiere for the film was held at midnight – a Terronez idea, of course. Usually at these things, there were several limousines dropping off the stars at the red carpet, so they could all slowly stroll into the theater.

But for this premiere, there was only one white limousine. TV camera crews, photographers, paparazzis and fans all scurried to snap glamorous shots of Jeffrey Terronez in his silky white PJs and dark sunglasses and Emerlinde in her long white gown and black shades.

Aimee Breeze, Entertainment Reporter for *Talent Tonight*, stuck a microphone in front of the special-effects whiz and said, "We're here with Jeffrey Terronez, the self-styled Wizard of Ooze. Jeffrey, your contributions to horror films are legendary. What can we expect to see in this new release of yours?"

Terronez smiled for the camera. "I raised the bar of violence even more with this one. It will be my goriest, most realistic production yet."

Aimee flashed a bleached-teeth smile to the camera. "Anything else you'd like to add?"

"Yes." Terronez kept smiling. "To those of you who think special effects are taking over today's horror films, I say: You're exactly right. Enjoy." He then gently took his sister's hand and walked with her into the theater.

BONUS:
Interview with the Queen of the Scream Queens:
LINNEA QUIGLEY
by Michael McCarty

Reprinted by permission from *Modern Mythmakers:*
35 Interviews with Horror and Science Fiction
Writers and Filmmakers
Crystal Lake Publishing, 2015)

Linnea Quigley is one of the horror industry's most beloved "scream queens". She has made close to one hundred movies, has appeared in *Fangoria* Magazine a number of times and is still a big draw at horror conventions across the country. She was ranked number nine on *Maxim* Magazine's 'Hottest Women of Horror Movies" and course the star of *Linnea Quigley's Horror Workout.*

Linnea Quigley has starred in her share of horror cult classics such as *Return of the Living Dead, Night of the Demons, Hollywood Chainsaw Hookers, Sorority Babes in the Slimeball Bowl-O-Rama, Burial of the Rats, Beach Babes From Beyond, The Walking Dead Girls, The Barn, Bonehill Road, Clownado, Silent Night, Deadly Night,* (I have a warm spot in my heart, or elsewhere for her "Best Impaled-on-Antlers" performance in that film) *Nightmare Sisters* and *Girls Gone Dead.* Besides producing movies, she plays guitar and sings in the all-girl rock band, The Skirts. She was the first woman inducted into the Horror Hall of Fame by "Fangoria Magazine." This from a lady whose first big break in showbiz was acting in a toothpaste commercial.

She decided to move to Florida to be closer to her parents in the early 2000s. She currently lives in South Florida with her myriad pets and is a big supporter of animal rights.

Linnea Quigley is one of the biggest stars to cross the B-horror movie market. She has co-authored two books with Michael McCarty, *Night of the Scream Queen* and *Return of the Scream Queen,*

153

both available as ebooks and trade paperbacks. She is queen of the B's--long live the queen! Her websites are: www.linneaquigley.net, www.myspace.com/originaltrash
and   www.linneaquigleycircle.com

This interview was done via the phone from Linnea's manager Danna Taylor's office.

How did you go from living in Davenport, Iowa to becoming one of Hollywood's most successful "scream queens"?

LINNEA QUIGLEY: Anybody that goes to L.A. gets sucked into the acting trap and then it's like, you're working at some lousy job or something and everybody goes, "Oh you should be an actress or a model, you're very glamorous." You're more attainable than in Iowa, so I went for it! I started getting modeling gigs and I took acting classes and even though I was real shy I ended up doing OK and I was totally shocked that it actually all happened.

You made close to a hundred films--that is amazing for someone who "accidentally fell into acting." At which point did you decide you enjoyed it and wanted to pursue a career in moviemaking?

LINNEA: I never thought there would be a way for me, it seemed like it was so unattainable. I was born in Iowa. I didn't think I was pretty enough, I was shy. I didn't think I would be able to utter any words or do anything. I wished and wished--it took a lot of conquering my fears--this business is pretty rough on people. In the beginning it was scary. I started out doing extras work, one liners and things like that and learned all about the business. I would help out on different things and learn as much as I could.

Was there an early movie, when you saw yourself on the screen and said, "I'm a professional actress now--I finally made it?"

LINNEA: Did you read my old diaries? (laughs). One of the first movies that I spoke in, *Fairy Tales*, I remember writing down in my diary: "Oh my God, I am a star now. I'm in a movie, I went to a theater to see it." It wasn't much of a part. To me, "this is it."

In *Return of the Living Dead*, when you became a zombie, the make-up effect they used on you, looks like it was a mask with an open mouth. Did you have a hard time biting people when you probably couldn't move your mouth?

LINNEA: It was horrible. There were two masks made. Dan (Author's Note: Dan O'Bannon, the director and co-screenwriter, passed away on December 17, 2009) had Kenny Myers make them. For the close-up, the mask was way down. They had it when I was going to bite the people, the "Send more cops" scenes and such. They used the mask for the close-ups. He wanted the mask really exaggerated.

In *Return of the Living Dead*, you stripped on top of a crypt that was lit by burning torches and was covered in sawdust that was supposed to be Spanish moss. Were you worried about something catching fire?

LINNEA: No (laughs). But I was getting very dizzy because the torches were those sulfuric acid torches they use when there is an accident (road flares). The fumes from the torches were going right up into my face. We did take after take and they lit them and those fumes were brutal.

In the last half of *Return of the Living Dead*, you portrayed a naked zombie in the rain. Was that uncomfortable?

LINNEA: Yes. It was horrible. It was very cold out. L.A. gets cold at night, the temperature drops like crazy. I was freezing. I couldn't sit down because the makeup would rub off. I couldn't put a towel around me because the makeup would rub off. It was just horrible.

What was it like working on the original *Night of the Demons*?

LINNEA: I kept telling them I won't go up for the role because the cast was all teenagers and I was sick of going to the interviews and they wanted someone who was twelve (laughs). It was weird because everyone was eighteen. I didn't know how to say some of the words in the script, like "wuss," I kept saying "wus."

Were you in your twenties then?

LINNEA: Yeah. There was a huge age gap between us.

Let's talk about the remake of *Night of the Demon*. What can you tell us about it?

LINNEA: It is many years later and everybody is wearing less clothing (laughs)--oh no, that doesn't happen (laughs). It is a little creepier, there is a lot more money to work with. The writers, the director, everybody is great. Kevin (S. Tenney--the director of the original) approved it--that is a good thing because most people wouldn't want a remake to be out there and be awful. I think people will be happy with the remake. I always hate it when people go, "they shouldn't have done a remake."

Besides the *Night of the Demons* remake. What else are you working on?

LINNEA: *Post Mortem America, 2021* – that is going to be real kick-ass, that should be put out very soon. There are a bunch of other ones which are in production. I am doing a lot of writing and producing. I co-produced *Vampire Theater*, which is coming out any day now on DVD. *The Notorious Colonel Steel* just came out and *Salvage Streets* was re-released as a special edition and so was *Hollywood Chainsaw Hookers* (Twentieth anniversary, see interview with Fred Olen Ray).

I also did a scream track for a song called "scream queen" by a band called Rip Snorter. It is going to rock!

What's your secret for continuing to look so good? Do your zombie workouts have anything to do with that?

LINNEA: Yes (laughs). I must say, living in California though is the best treatment for anyone-- that is one of the best workouts.

What is your opinion of CGI (computer generated images) in genre films?

LINNEA: I don't like them. I remember watching *Terminator 2* and that was the first time I really ever saw CGI effects. It was like "ugh!" It just wrecks the movie for me.

Any films you regret making and why?

LINNEA: No, because it got me where I was going. Sometimes now, I look back at mainly how I was treated, and I think, Danna Taylor who is my manager--she is amazing, she does things right. Everybody else just kind of sent me out to the wolves --they didn't care what I'd be doing or if I'd be cold or the food I'd eat or anything. The others were so artificial type of people. Back to the question, I regret that I worked on films where they were not treating me or paying me right.

Any projects you regret not making?

LINNEA: Not really. There were films I could have done, but couldn't due to circumstances.

Which films are you the most proud of?

LINNEA: Of course, *Return of the Living Dead*--the way it came out and everything. *Night of the Demons* both the original and remake, I am excited, plus it's really weird seeing another Suzanne that is going to be weird (the character she played in the original, the role in the remake is played by Bobbi Sue Luther), it makes you realize how much things have evolved and how long I have been in the film business--whoa--scary (laughs). I liked doing *Hollywood Chainsaw Hookers*. There are so many. *Hoodoo for Voodoo* was fun. *Treasure of the Moon Goddess* was a blast. *Savage Streets* for me was a hard part. Everybody says, "You didn't have any lines" --it was really hard to do, it was challenge--not being able to make any kind of noise.

This one I am doing with Cameron Scott, *Post Mortem America, 2021* --it is a really great part, the weird thing is, I met him when he was sixteen. A lot of years later, he always wanted to make a movie and he did it. That is amazing.

Do you still have copies of all of them?

LINNEA: No, some I don't, I need to find them. A lot of them are hard to find. A lot of them are, "that was a great performance," but I haven't even seen it--I am not sure if it is released or how to get hold of it.

Some of those '80 movies that came out on video aren't available on DVD or Blu-Ray.

LINNEA: I know it. Those movies like *Sorority Babes in the Slimeball Bowl-A-Rama*--I liked too, it was fun. The crew was like family, it was a blast. It is so different now. It isn't like a family anymore, because there are so many production companies.

You are also a producer, you were the executive producer for "Creepozoids." "Dead End" (producer), "The Girl I Want" (co-producer), "Linnea Quigley's Horror Workout" (associate producer) and "Murder Weapon" (producer). How did that come about?

LINNEA: I really had more hands-on. It came about because I was working with David DeCoteau (the director of such films as "Sorority Babes in the Slimeball Bowl-A-Rama" and "Creepozoids") a lot and he asked me to co-produce and I said "yeah." I jumped on it because I always wanted to do something besides acting.

You've spoken of your desire to produce films, if you had an unlimited budget, what kind of film would you make?

LINNEA: Cynthia Garris (director Mick Garris' wife) and I had written a screenplay for a scary movie, kind of the old scary movie type about saving animals in a lab. It was pretty dark, a lot of action, things like that going on. It was a good script, as I remember. We tried at the time, to go to a few places--it was really hard at that time, they were doing movies mostly for two million or down to sixty thousand. I still have the synopsis and everything.

Not many people know you are a writer too. You wrote the books *Bio & Chainsaws, I'm Screaming as Fast as I can, Skin* and co-written the novels *Night of the Scream Queen* and *Return of the Scream Queen* with me.

LINNEA: They were fun to do.

You also had parts in *Innocent Blood*, where you played a nurse that gets sprayed with Don Rickle's blood. *Nightmare on Elm Street 4: The Dream Master.* Tell us about working on the fourth *Nightmare* film.

LINNEA: I played the soul coming out of Freddy's chest. I got engaged after that (to make-up artist Steve Johnson--who also did the makeup effects for the original *Night of the Demons*--they are now divorced.) The stunt went wrong, the huge Freddy statue fell. We almost got killed. The one lady working the head, the puppeteer (Mecki Heussen) fell onto concrete, she was probably about three stories up.

You shot *Sorority Babes in the Slimeball Bowl-A-Rama* in a bowling alley, where at?

LINNEA: That movie was directed by David DeCoteau. We shot it in San Marcos (California), at an all-night bowling alley. It was a lot of fun to do.

159

Have you ever appeared in *Playboy* magazine?

LINNEA: Three times: The "Girls of Rock N Roll," a dancing one and "B-Movie Queens" pictorials.

How long did it take for the makeup artists to apply body paint in *Hollywood Chainsaw Hookers*?

LINNEA: Eleven hours with three people. They thought it would only take three hours and then they had to keep calling in people. I even called my ex-husband (special effects wizard Steve Johnson). It was ridiculous. It was a very long day.

Did you like the way the effect came out on the film?

LINNEA: Oh yeah. The effect was great but standing there for that long was horrible. I get very fidgety.

What was it like working with low-budget guru director Fred Olen Ray in **Hollywood Chainsaw Hookers** (which he wrote and directed) and *Jack-O*? (which he wrote the story for)?"

LINNEA: Interesting. He's got a very sarcastic way of doing things. He keeps things moving along. He knows what he's doing. He was fun.

One of your co-stars in *Hollywood Chainsaw Hookers* is Michelle Bauer. You've done a number of films with this "scream queen". What is Michelle Bauer like on and off screen?

LINNEA: She is great, she is amazing. It is so much fun working with her because she is so down-to-earth. She is never, "I am a star." She is just a happy, go watch football and hangout type person.

How did you get involved with animal rights?

LINNEA: I got involved after watching this news documentary when I was twenty-one years old. The show was about the experiments they do on animals. Those images burned into my brain. I had to help out after that.

Why do you think guys are attracted to "scream queens" so much?

LINNEA: I don't know. Some of the conventions girls call themselves "scream queens" but they haven't done any movies, what I'd consider "scream queen" movies. It has changed a lot, but there haven't been a whole lot of new "scream queens" that you heard about, they have the girl from *Saw* (Leigh Whannel who also co-wrote the movie).

But they haven't really done any movies.

DANNA & LINNEA: Right.

You were talking about *Saw*. What is your take on the current popularity of extreme horror films like *Hostel* and the *Saw* movies?

LINNEA: I think it is going back *to Last House on the Left*--things like that. Where movies were really bloody and realistic. They are concentrating a lot on torturing women. It is the monster next door opposed to the monster from beyond.

Any role or part you wouldn't take and why?

DANNA: We turn them down on a daily basis.

Really?

LINNEA: I am surprised. I look at the scripts and go, "Oh my God." We hear so and so is going to do that movie and it was

161

offered to us because they had read it. The script is really bad.

DANNA: A lot people seem to make movies that are just about how many ways can we get X person naked, beaten and cut up and repeatedly raped. There is no story to it, it is a two-hour rape scene and what is the point of that? That is what we turn down.

Any unfulfilled fantasy about working with big name stars or directors?

DANNA: She has always wanted to work with Rob Zombie.

LINNEA: Yeah, Rob Zombie. Quentin Tarantino. Quentin and I had the same manager for years and then he got big, the lady who manages him--Cathryn James, she got him there.

Robert Rodriguez (the director of such movies as *From Dusk till Dawn, Planet Terror* and the *Machete* movies) would be great to work with.

I'd like to work with Mick Garris again. I've known Mick and Cynthia Garris for so long. I have a tape--I have to change it over to DVD. When Mick was struggling to get by, his wife was teaching aerobics classes. Mick wanted to be a moviemaker, he wrote a little something--we all had little parts in it. It is based on a true story of his, it was more comedy. I'd love to work with him--because he's a great guy.

Cheech and Chong are making a comeback and you appeared in two of their films *Nice Dreams* and *Still Smokin'*. Are they as wild and crazy as in their movies? What was it like being on the set with them?

LINNEA: Cheech is really a nice, smart guy. Tommy Chong, I don't know that well, he is more quiet.

Cheech is really into his career, a happy guy, a genuine person. It is so cool that he broke that barrier and got onto *Nash Bridges*.

Any advice to ladies looking to break into the horror film field?

LINNEA: You got to trust your gut feeling. There are a lot of people I've helped and given advice to, but they don't follow it--you really got to do things--and they don't. You get tired of repeating yourself again and again.

And get everything in writing. Get to the bank with them, maybe bring a taser if you have to (laughs). Turn into the psycho that you are playing (laughs). Tell them you want your money or you are calling in Danna (laughs). There is a lot of sweeping involved.

DANNA: Yes, I got to sweep up the mess (laughs).

Last words?

LINNEA: I'm going to get out of Florida and back to California. Also, I want people not to be so hard on themselves if they are in this business. There will be people who will try to take you down because they are going down. You've just got to be careful of that. You can get very upset about it. You've just got to keep your confidence and be around people that are positive and good.

Mini Graphic Novel and Art:

Desiree Starr Behind the Scenes of

Vampire Vixens from Outer Space

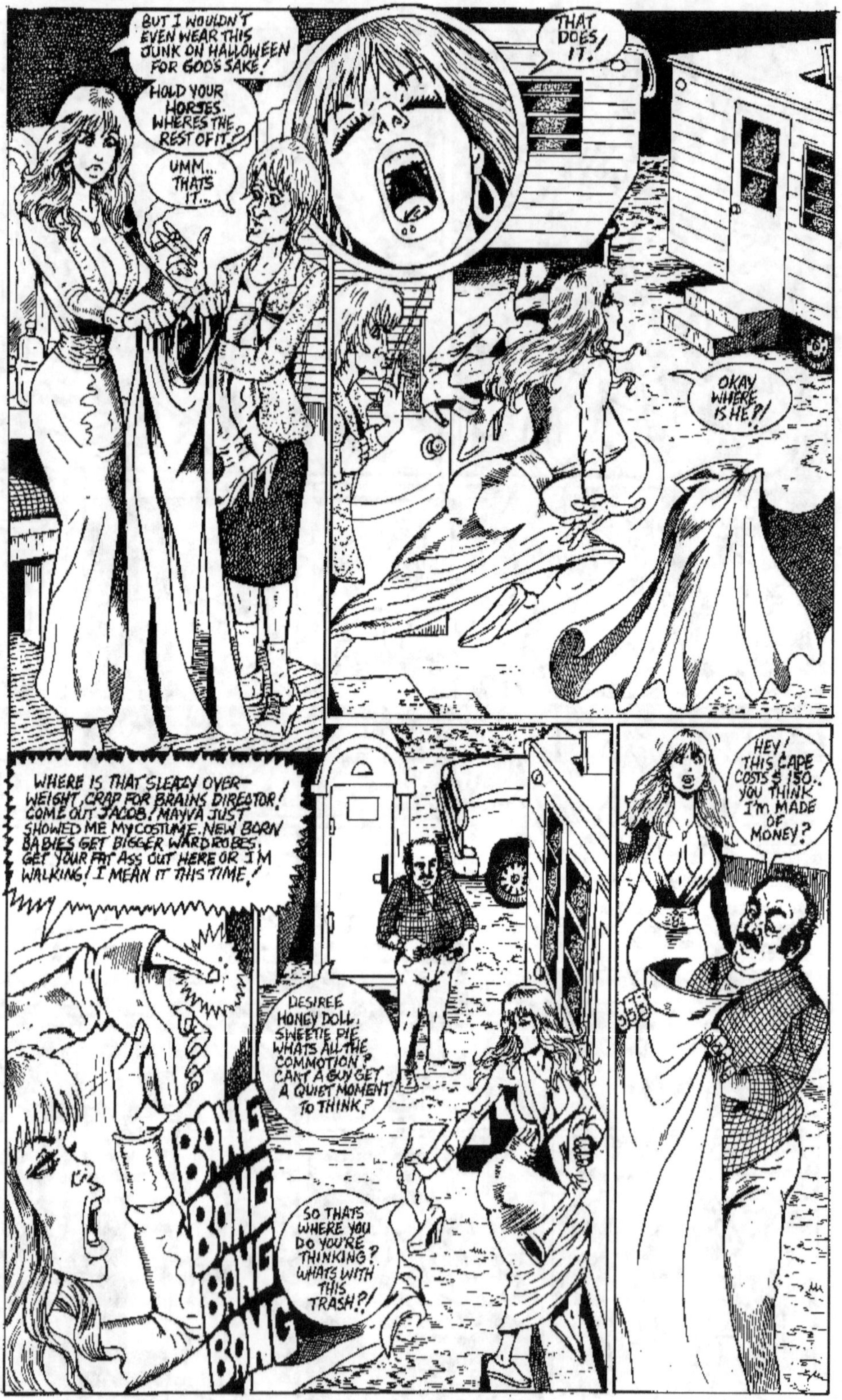

Look for us wherever books are sold.

If you thought *this book* was cool, check out these other titles from the #1 source for the best in independent horror fiction, Black Bed Sheet Books
www.blackbedsheetbooks.com

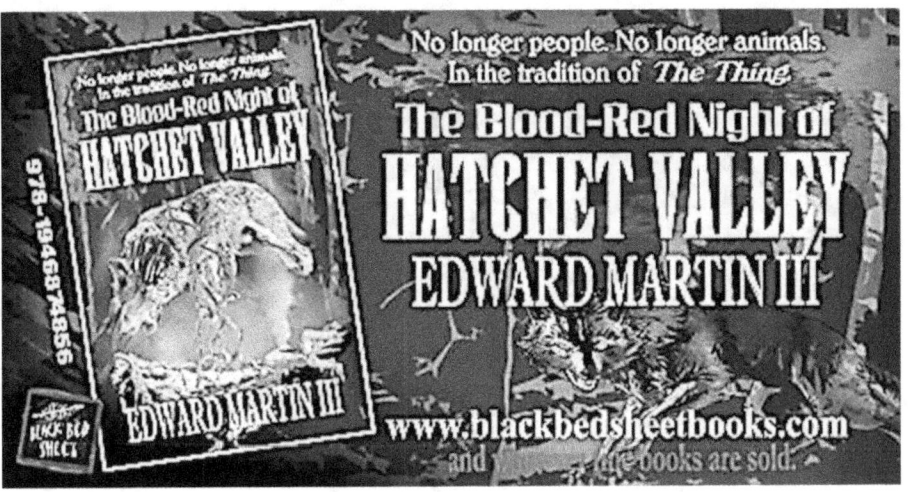

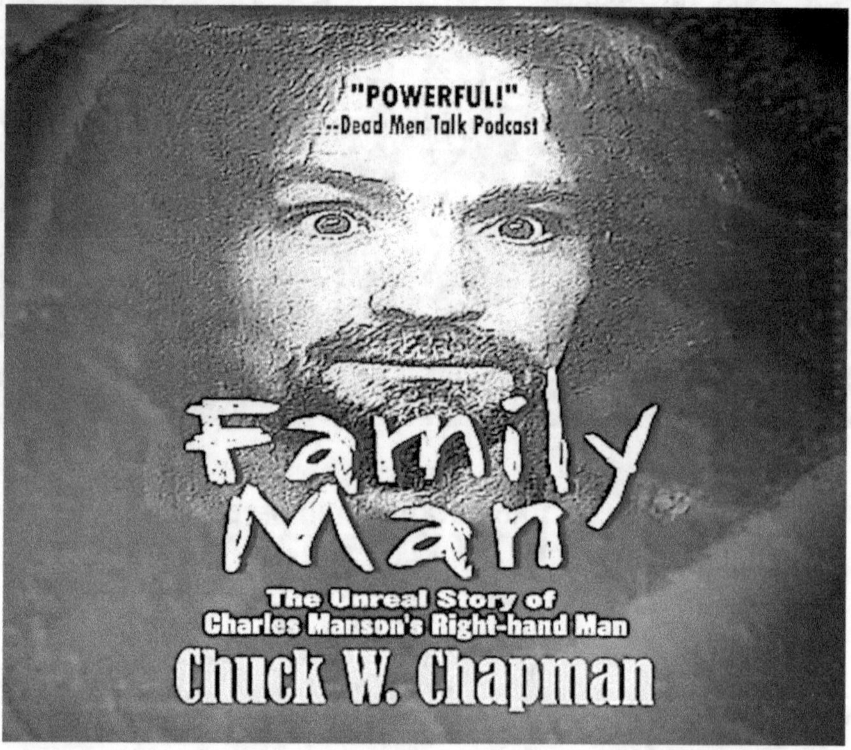

"CHOPHOUSE makes me SCREAM!"
--Linnea Quigley

Chophouse by Horns (Terry Horns)
Look for this slasher gem everywhere
books are sold!

www.ingramcontent.com/pod-product-compliance
Lightning Source LLC
Chambersburg PA
CBHW070517260626
47161CB00004B/1573